Smelling Herself

SMELLING HERSELF

A NOVEL

TERRIS MCMAHAN GRIMES

Createspace Independent Publishing Platform
ISBN: 978-1492300540
Library of Congress Control Number: 2013916510

Cover design by Contessa Cooper, www.contessalouise.com and Shawn Hansen, IndieBookMarketer.com.

Cover art by Kathy Gold

ACKNOWLEDGMENTS

Dedicated to
Martha Tate-Glass,
sister-friend and mentor

Albert Schweitzer once said "At times our own light goes out and is rekindled by a spark from another person." Jacquelyn Turner Banks, Warren Bonta, and Lawrence Kasparowitz each provided that spark that kept my light burning. I want to express my sincere gratitude for their unflagging support and the many hours they spent reading and critiquing my many drafts.

This book wouldn't have been possible without the assistance of an "Emergency Response" team of editors. I am grateful for editorial expertise and assistance provided by:

Martine Bellen Literary Services, http://bookdoctorbellen.com

Laura Silverman, www.elance.com/s/ljsilverman1

Kenneth W. Umbach, Ph.D., www.umbachconsulting.com

CHAPTER 1

Growing titties takes focus.

With all my measuring, exercising, and secret application of specially-formulated, 100 percent guaranteed creams that I ordered with my own money, using one of those coupons on the back of Mama's *Jive* magazine, I had a lot on my mind. So, it took me a while to figure out what was going on with Jessie Mae.

And once I did, I wished to God I didn't know.

We weren't Ozzie and Harriet or anything like that, but none of the families living in Chestnut Court projects in 1964 were. We were just a plain ol' family with a daddy who went to work early in the morning carrying a lunch pail, and who came home after dark all covered in creosote, a mama who worked for a white family up in the Oakland hills, and two girls, me and my sister Chantelle. She was thirteen. I was eleven.

A plain ol' family. At least we were until Jessie Mae moved into the apartment over ours and everything happened. You may be wondering what "everything" was. I'll get to that. First, let me explain a few things so you can understand what I did, what I didn't do, and why.

I had gotten tired of waiting for my titties to show up on their own, so I decided to grow me some. I didn't need great, big, hoochie-coochie mamas like Chantelle's. Some little ones would have been just fine. I needed to show Chantelle that she wasn't the only one who could grow them. She and I used to be best friends, ever. It didn't matter that we were sisters, or even that she was two years older than me. We were tight. We did everything together. We kept one another's secrets. But, when Chantelle began to fill out, she got all fast, and started thinking she was too grown for me. She started hanging out with people like Charlesetta, and suddenly, boys became so—necessary. The worst part was, she started talking about me behind my back, calling me a baby, saying I peed the bed—mess like that. So, titties weighed heavily on my mind. If there had been the remotest chance that I could have gotten some for Christmas, they would have been on the top of my list.

I'm not trying to make excuses, or anything, for all the stuff that happened. I know I messed up. I know things probably wouldn't have turned out the way they did if I had done something sooner. But, like I said, I had a lot on my mind.

Jessie Mae was dark skinned and as skinny as Bony Maronie. Her short hair didn't take to the hot comb, and every time I saw her, it was standing up on her head like a hedge. She was the quietest li'l thing I ever saw, and it was some time before I even got to talk to her. The only thing I knew about Jessie Mae was she was around the same age as Chantelle, and she was as country as smoked ham.

She didn't show her face unless she was with her mama, Lee Ann, when they went to the washhouse across the parking lot from our building, or when the Sheik, Lee Ann's boyfriend, took them out evangelizing. Jessie Mae scurried about like a little mouse. Getting off the bus with her mama and the Sheik—scurry, scurry inside the apartment. Going from their apartment to the washhouse—scurry there, scurry back again. One day Mama sent me to the washhouse, and Jessie Mae and her mama were there. Jessie Mae held her head down the entire time. She never looked up once.

On weekends Mama ran a little side business doing people's hair in the kitchen. Eventually I was able to pick up a little information about Jessie Mae and her jacked up family from people's loose talk as they sat in front of the kitchen stove getting their press and curls. According to the gossip, Jessie Mae's mother, Lee Ann, had been bumping around West Oakland for years, from one housecleaning job to another, from one man to another. Because the poor child wasn't too bright, she was always going for the okey doke. They said if you asked Lee Ann to choose between a pile of gold bars and the same size pile of pancakes, she would choose the pancakes because they were easier to carry.

She met the Sheik when he used to be a penny-ante pimp. He tried to teach Lee Ann to be a ho, but she kept losing the money or forgetting to ask for it at all, and that didn't work out too well. The Sheik looked around for another line of work and decided to open a church. Lee Ann became one of his apostles or something. The Sheik kept after Lee Ann to send for Jessie Mae from someplace down south where she had been happily living her life with her grandmother since the day she was born. Finally Lee Ann did.

Jessie Mae had never lived with Lee Ann and didn't know anything about her. She knew even less about the Sheik. And, let me tell you, if she had known what she was in for, I am certain she would have hidden in the corn crib or the cotton gin or whatever places they have down South to hide in, before she would have let them put her on a train and send her to him.

The neighborhood kids gave the Sheik his name because of the long robes and turbans he always wore. He called himself a bishop. Bishop Willie Nathan of the New Nubian Church of Enlightenment. Funniest church anybody ever saw. His congregation was Lee Ann and Jessie Mae. His pulpit, when he wasn't going door to door, was down on Tenth Street in front of Housewives' Market, where he preached to the taxi drivers waiting to take people places, the wino or two who staggered by, and people at the bus stop.

I saw him down there, with my own two eyes, one Friday when

me and Chantelle went with Mama to pick up some buffalo fish at Marino Brothers.

Mama pinched us for giggling. "Don't you all laugh," she warned. "You never know how the Lord's gonna come back."

On the off chance that the Lord might choose to come back as the most ludicrous, most ridiculous fool imaginable, I dropped a quarter in the basket at the Sheik's feet. Chantelle deposited seventeen cents.

The time came when I sure wished I had that money back.

One evening before Jessie Mae got there, the Sheik came to our apartment on one of his door-to-door evangelical sweeps. Daddy refused to let him in. "Just another Negro from Mississippi trying to get paid," he said. But sometimes Mama was kindhearted. She stood at the door and listened to the Sheik's cockeyed sermon, nodding, voicing a random "Amen" now and then as the Sheik preached and quoted the Bible, getting everything all mixed up. Lee Ann just stood there, a tambourine dangling from her hand. I kept my head down as the Sheik eyed me and Chantelle.

Sometimes I would hear Jessie Mae upstairs getting whuppins. I didn't pay that much attention, then. As I told you, I had a lot on my mind. Besides, everybody got their behinds beat once in a while—especially my sister Chantelle. Even me. That's what it cost being a kid. Whuppins were like kid taxes we paid with our behinds. We didn't get "spankings" either. Spankings were what weak, little white kids up in the hills got. We were rough and tough flatland kids who walked the two miles from overcrowded project apartments to Jack London Square just to throw rocks in the water. Our mamas wrapped extension cords around their hands or made us strip switches from the trees outside our bedroom windows, and they used them to leave welts on our bare arms and legs, make us do holy dances, shout out the Lord's name, and make promises we knew we couldn't keep.

Our people came from places like Mississippi, Arkansas, and Alabama. I used to think those were the states where it was legal to kill off your bad kids because our mamas were always saying they'd rather kill us than have somebody else do it. It seemed that if they didn't whup us, and nobody killed us, then we had no choice but to grow up to be no good. We'd end up walking San Pablo Avenue all glassy eyed, in some big ol' lopsided wig, with our skirts hiked up over our behinds. And the shortest, most direct path to San Pablo Avenue was by way of eye-rolling, back-talking, correcting, and disrespecting grown people, stealing money out of our mamas' purses that they'd put right there on the table next to their beds, taking their boyfriends, and—the unholiest of unholies—talking their business.

I couldn't imagine Jessie Mae doing any of those things. Like I said, she was the quietest li'l somethin' I ever saw—except when she was getting a whuppin.

CHAPTER 2

Sam Cooke was dead.

Over the weekend some hoochie-coochie woman had shot him down. That was all anybody had talked about at school.

Dinner dishes had been washed and put away. Mama, Chantelle, and I sat around the table talking. But Chantelle could hardly choke out a word. Sam Cooke was dead and she was grieving. Her grief seemed to increase when Mama dumped a pile of laundry on the table and told us to get to folding. Chantelle started boo-hooing, getting snot all over everything. She sounded like she was gargling spit and trying to yodel at the same time.

I shot a glance her way. I was trying to warn her that the barometric pressure had changed and lightning was about to strike. I glanced over at the couch where Daddy sat working on one of his crossword puzzles. *Do something, Daddy!* He was crazy about Sam Cooke, too, and I thought he was blinking a lot, like something was in his eye. He was also oblivious to the storm clouds gathering above us. Just as I was about to give up all hope, Daddy looked me dead in the eye and said, "Somnambulist. You have ten seconds."

"Daddy, not now," I whispered. "Chantelle—"

"Nine . . ."

"Sleepwalker!"

"Eight . . ."

"Uh, uh . . . an abnormal condition of sleep in which motor acts such as walking are performed"

With a wink at me, Daddy returned to his crossword.

"Daddy, help!" I whispered as loud as I dared. But he didn't hear me.

Mama looked at Chantelle, shook her head, and said, "Sam Cooke had a wife." She said it like a wife was all anybody needed in this life. "He had a wife," Mama repeated, "and he shouldn't been out messing around in the first place."

That only made Chantelle worse. Sam Cooke was dead, her heart was breaking, and Mama didn't even care.

Mama shook a towel, making it crack like a whip. I jumped. Mama folded the towel in three quick motions. She eyed my pile of laundry and then Chantelle's. My pile was getting smaller, Chantelle's wasn't.

Mama picked up another towel and snapped it. She said, "You better stop all that mess, or I'll give you something to cry for."

It was obvious that Chantelle was cruisin' for a bruisin', but I couldn't understand why. She should have gone ahead and got the folding over with, instead of baiting Mama. Maybe, I thought, it was just her destiny. That child got more whuppins than any self-respecting, thirteen-year-old I ever knew. I, on the other hand, was so scared of whuppins that I would do just about anything to avoid one. I learned early on to mind, to do what Mama and Daddy told me. I even thought up ways to be good and to get noticed at it. Some people—I won't mention names—used to call me a kiss ass. Oh well, I yam what I yam. Toot, toot.

I knew what I was doing. I had to mind. I didn't have that much going for me. I wasn't cute or a cripple or anything, and I wasn't light skinned. I did have what the old ladies called a "head full of hair." It wasn't good hair, but it was long, falling down my back when Mama took a hot comb to it. My nickname was Punkin. That should tell you something. Chantelle, on the other hand, was cute. She had good hair and she was light skinned. Her nickname was Peaches. Get the picture? But poor "Peaches" wasn't too good at arithmetic. She thought cute bought her way more than it actually did. That usually ended up costing her. Those light-colored eyes didn't cut anything with Mama. Besides, Chantelle's hair was only kind'a good—Mama still had to press it with a warm comb.

Outside somebody was trying to sing Sam Cooke's "You Send Me."

Yoo-o-o-o send me.

He was off key and sounded like he was yodeling, too.

Yoo-o-o-o send me.

That really set Chantelle off, and she yodeled even louder. Mama snapped another towel, raised a brow, and looked at Chantelle from the corner of her eye.

With that gesture, she sucked all the air out of the room. It seemed to be shrinking, getting tighter, warmer. I knew what was coming. I didn't know if I could stand seeing the child get skinned again.

I got up and grabbed my pile of unfolded laundry, including in it as much of Chantelle's pile as I could without Mama noticing.

"Where you going?" Mama demanded.

"The bedroom. I'll finish folding in there. Chantelle's *bumptiousness* is getting on my nerves."

Daddy looked up and winked at me. Mama sighed the way you do when you're surrounded by fools. "Have you set the beans to soaking for tomorrow?"

"Yes, ma'am," I said.

Mama went down her list of chores until she got to Chantelle's.

"Chantelle, you mop the kitchen?"

Chantelle hadn't touched a mop and Mama knew it, Daddy knew it, the people down the block and round the corner knew it. Chantelle was really yodeling now. I edged my foot over under the table and nudged her, trying to remind her that I'd mopped it for her. She looked up into my blank face and just sat there like a dummy staring at me. I was really getting worried, until she finally said, "Uh . . . yes?" like she was guessing on a test, which maybe she was. Mama looked at me. I willed my face to stay blank. I wasn't going to take a whuppin for Chantelle under any circumstances.

Mama knew I'd mopped the floor for Chantelle, but she said, "Okay, Bernadine, you can go on."

The extension cord was Mama's symbol of authority, her mace, and her sword. She always kept it within reach. That evening she had been sitting with it in her lap. Daddy got up to change the television channel. He was messing with the rabbit ears.

Get out'a here while you got the chance.

I was almost out of the room when I made the mistake of turning around to see what was happening, and got turned into a pillar of salt. Just then Mama decided she'd had enough of Chantelle. She had wrapped the cord around her hand a couple of times, and popped Chantelle good, before the stupid thing knew what was happening. The end of the cord cut into Chantelle's shoulder, close to her neck, and I flinched like Mama had hit me. I knew from experience that type of lick would leave a U-shape welt that would swell into a water-filled sack, then dry up and scab over, eventually leaving a scar that would look like somebody had branded her with a little lucky horseshoe.

Chantelle screamed and threw up her arms like she was in church getting happy. The second lick caught her wrist, the cord coiling around it like a snake.

I started to hum. I couldn't help it; that's what I do when I'm scared. I crossed my legs and danced in place, trying not to do that other thing I do when I'm scared.

Mama usually measured out her whuppins the way she measured out a dose of Pepto-Bismol. She was cool, calm, and collected about it. But something was wrong. Mama was beating Chantelle like she was a run-away slave.

Chantelle knew better, but she tried to run. The rules of getting a whuppin are not written down anywhere; still, everybody knows them. One of them is once you try to run all bets are off. Mama grabbed Chantelle by the hair without missing a lick.

It was forty days and forty nights before Daddy said anything.

"You don't have to beat the child like that," he finally said.

Mama got in another lick before Daddy grabbed her arm.

"You hear me, Vondra; don't be beating that child like she's a dog or something."

Mama jerked away. She was breathing hard and just itching to hit Chantelle one more lick. Chantelle stomped off to the kitchen. I could hear her throwing up in the sink. Mama yelled after her, "You bring your li'l fast ass back here and get these clothes up off the floor!" I stood there, arms full of laundry, trying to figure out what was going on, why Mama was so worked up. And Chantelle, she knew better. Why was she pushing Mama way past the butt whuppin limit?

Mama turned on Daddy. "You don't have a clue, Alex. Just stay out of this. Don't be interfering between me and my girls."

Daddy said, "They're my children too, Vonnie. I work and support them. They carry my name."

But Mama stomped off to the bedroom before he even finished.

Daddy avoided looking at me. He turned his face away like he was ashamed. I wanted to tell him it was okay; I didn't care one bit. It was okay if he wasn't the daddy I came from; he was still my real daddy, my only daddy. Anyway, Chantelle had already told me the secret—Mama had Chantelle with a man called Big Josh, and I came along a couple of years later. But that was past history. I could care less about Big Josh, whoever he was. He was a stranger to me and certainly not my daddy. I didn't say anything out loud, though; instead, I went to me and Chantelle's room, closed the door, and wedged the back of a chair under the knob. Then I took off my panties, rolled them up in some newspaper, and hid the package under my bed. I would wait until everybody was asleep, then sneak out to the back landing, and drop it down the garbage chute. At least it wasn't as bad as it used to be. My panties were just a little soggy. Nothing had run down my leg. My shoes weren't full of pee. That was progress.

It was cold outside, but I opened the window a crack, anyway, to keep the room from stinking up. I stood there looking down at Chestnut Street. The Counts Boys were working on the ol' bread truck they were trying to fix up and turn into a hippie van. They had a long way to go as far as I could see. Some little kids playing a war game darted between parked cars, making pow-pow noises.

I stayed there looking down. I thought about checking to see if my titties had grown any, but I didn't want to jinx them by checking right after something bad had happened.

After a while I saw the Sheik and Lee Ann come around the corner from West Grand Avenue, where they must have gotten off the Number 88 bus. Jessie Mae trudged behind them, struggling with a couple of heavy shopping bags. They both hauled bags, Jessie Mae and her mother that is, not the Sheik. He sauntered along in front, clutching a long stick like he could part water or something, his robes and multicolored scarves writhing in the wind.

Jessie Mae wore a pair of saddle oxfords with no socks. They must have been too tight because somebody had cut holes in them to give her baby toes some room. All she had on to protect her body from the winter wind was a cotton dress and a thin sweater. From where I stood, she looked sad and confused like she sure could have used a grandmother, a sister, or a friend.

The Sheik's little caravan crossed the street making its way to our shared entrance. Viola Jackson and her bad-ass little grandkids lived on the ground floor in 1B, we were in the middle in apartment 2B, and the Sheik and them were on the top floor in 3B. Miss Viola was whuppin somebody and they all were running around down there screaming and cussing—Miss Viola included. I took off my shoe and bammed on the floor, so they would know somebody in this world needed some peace and quiet.

I returned to the window and watched as Jessie dragged to a stop and let the heavy bags drop at her feet. Her hands crept to the small of her back, and she arched it, craning her neck the way old women do. She was all reared back like that when our eyes met. I held up my hand, palm outward. Jessie Mae shot a quick glance at the Sheik before returning my salute.

The Sheik whirled around in a flash of sashes and rags, catching Jessie with her hand still in the air. Never in my life have I seen anything as pitiful as the look on her face when she realized she'd gotten caught. In two steps the Sheik was on her, had drawn back his hand, and slapped her across her thin face. Her mama's hand shot to her own mouth like she could taste the blow, but the Sheik had her so cowed she didn't say anything, and she didn't do anything either.

Mama whupped us, but she sure didn't let anybody else lay a hand on us. She would have been all over the Sheik. She would have whupped his ass until it roped like okra and prayed on it afterwards. Daddy would have shot him, plain and simple. At that very moment I could have killed the Sheik myself. I could have ripped off his arm and beat him silly with it; I could have dashed gasoline in his face and thrown a match after it; I could have gouged his eyes out and stomped them to jelly. But Lee Ann and Jessie Mae just stood there like they were playing freeze tag. The Sheik strode back to the front of their little procession and marched off.

Jessie Mae didn't so much bend down to pick up her bags as she sagged until her hands made contact with the string handles. Then she drew herself up and started off behind her mother and the Sheik, taking care not to get caught looking up again. Just before the Sheik disappeared into our entrance, he lifted his head, enough for me to see that he was smiling. I flipped him the finger, and I didn't care if he saw it, either. God, did I hate him. It was a feeling so strong it changed the color of my pee for an entire week.

CHAPTER 3

I didn't see much of Jessie Mae after that. She wasn't among the groups of kids ambling through puddles in the mornings on the way to school, or straggling home in the afternoons. Sometimes I heard her and Lee Ann scurrying around upstairs. Once I saw them going to the washhouse, but Jessie Mae was careful to hold her head down and I didn't get to wave or anything.

I did see her for a hot minute one day at school lined up with the little kids outside Miss Thompson's third grade class. She was twice as tall and twice as skinny as anybody in the line and probably twice as old. I intended to go over and say something to her, but the bell rang, and I had to get back to class before my teacher, Ol' Miz Bloom, had a hissy fit. But, the truth of the matter is, she looked like a fool in those saddle oxfords with no socks, towering over the little kids with that hangdog look of hers. I was ashamed to go over and speak to her. I didn't want any of my friends to see me talking to her. Now, after everything that happened, I am ashamed of myself for being so phony. There is nothing worse than a big, fat phony.

"She must be real dumb, big as she is, and still in the baby class," Brenda Mack, my fourth best friend said.

"Yeah," I said, "real dumb."

I took off running. I ran fast. I ran like I was trying to get away from something bad, like I was angry about something that I couldn't name. I slid into my seat just as the second bell rang.

Miz Bloom, announced that she had made a new seating chart, and told everyone to stand at the back of the room while she called out our names to tell us where we would sit. At the beginning of the school year we got to pick our own desks, but now Miz Bloom was putting us where *she* wanted. I stood against the wall with the rest of the class, waiting for Miz Bloom to call my name, hoping she didn't put me next to somebody who was stuck-up, or worse still, next to too many boys.

"María Cano," Miz Bloom began. "Carmelita López, Carlos Montoya, and Alejandro (she pronounced it "Al-jand-ro") Cruz, I want you to take a seat in the front row." Xolotl Meza was next, only Miz Bloom always called him "Ex-Lax Makes Ya," and laughed like Bozo or something each time she did. Nobody else ever laughed, except Deirdre Dean, Miz Bloom's pet. Deirdre was rich. Her mother worked for the phone company, and her daddy had a steady job doing something on the Bay Bridge. Deirdre told Miz Bloom everybody's business. She would tell on you if you farted, even if it was a little soft one that went "piff," that no one else heard.

Miz Bloom called "Jay-soos" next. Then she called "Mozzarella." Mozella made a face. Sometimes when she got on our nerves, we called her "funky, chunky, cheese girl." Corazon and Raul got put in the last seats in the second row. That left the rest of us.

Ol' Bad Richard Johnson was standing next to his buddy Darnell Davis. Ol' Bad Richard was the biggest kid in the class. They say he started kindergarten a whole year late because his grandmother was always too drunk to take him to school. Then he flunked the third grade. He must have been at least thirteen by then. He was a big thirteen, too, almost as big as a man, and he was *bad* in every sense of the word. He was one of the best fighters in the school. He knew all the dance moves. He could do the skate better even than James Brown. And cussing—he could out do a grown man. He could "ma fuck" with the best of them.

Some of the girls went on and on about how fine he was. Even Chantelle was stuck on him. She was always asking me, "You see

Richie today, wit' his fine self?" Or, "Tell Richie he didn't call last night like he said he would, and I stayed up all night long waiting." I just didn't see it myself—maybe because I didn't have titties, yet.

Richard leaned over and said something to Darnell, who nodded. Too bad they were standing next to Deirdre. Her arm shot straight up in the air. "Ooh, ooh, Miz Bloom, Miz Bloom," Deirdre called as she hopped from one foot to the other like she had to pee.

"What is it, Deirdre?" You could tell Miz Bloom didn't want to stop calling names, probably because she was scared she'd forget where she was and put two people in the same seat, maybe even three. Maybe stack them up to the ceiling. She was real old with gray hair and everything, and she was always forgetting things, little things, like what she was talking about a minute ago. Once she forgot what math pages we were supposed to do, and we kept turning in the same assignment for a month until Deirdre told on us.

"What is it?" Miz Bloom repeated.

"Can I come up there and tell you?"

"No, you *may* not."

"Okay. Well, Richard said you putting all the white kids in the front and all the Negroes in the back."

You could hear the entire class suck in its breath, and then it got real quiet waiting to see what Ol' Bad Richard was going to do. We didn't have white kids at Tompkins Elementary School. There were just us Negroes and the Spanish kids. The Spanish kids were actually Mexicans, Puerto Ricans, and a handful of Filipinos, but we called them Spanish out of courtesy. Some of the Negro kids had been grumbling among themselves, and now the Spanish kids were mad because they realized Miz Bloom was playing some weird kind of dozens with them, too.

Daddy always said give him a southern cracker any day, because a southern cracker is up front with his mess. The northern cracker was a whole 'nother story. Daddy said a northern cracker would throw a rock and try to hide his hand. It was hard to tell what Miz Bloom was doing.

Miz Bloom spun toward Richard and barked, "You come here!"

Too late. Richard was already on his mark, and as soon as he heard those words come out of her mouth, he bolted out the door. Boy was he fast. He was zigging and zagging like nobody's business. He didn't need to do all that, though. Wasn't no way Miz Bloom could'a caught him, even if she had been brave enough to try. Ol' Bad Richard wasn't scared. He just didn't want to have to hurt anybody.

Xolotl said, "Bump this," and walked real slow and real cool back to his old desk. We said "Ooh wee!" with our eyes, but we were too scared to move. Miz Bloom pretended not to notice Xolotl. The rest of us stayed against the back wall and waited for her to call our names and tell us where we belonged.

Miz Bloom put me all the way back in the last row. At least she didn't bother me back there, and I could look out the window all I wanted. She put Carmelita and Carlos right up front. All they could do was look up Miz Bloom's nose, and I'm telling you that was not a pretty sight.

Around three, when everybody was all squirmy because they wanted to get out of there, I put my head down on my desk and just stared out the window. A few scraggly seagulls picked at stuff on the playground left from lunch, and that's about all there was to see. I was about to turn away when I spotted the caravan—the Sheik, Lee Ann, and Jessie Mae walking in that line of theirs with the Sheik up front. They were picking up Jessie Mae early, probably so they could go down to Housewives' Market and get some evangelizing in before dinner. I should have been thinking "Poor Jessie Mae" but I wasn't. "I am so glad that isn't me," was my only thought.

I was about to turn around to see what all the snickering was about behind me in the "Negro Row" when I caught a glimpse of none other than Miss Chantelle. She knew she had no business at Tompkins. She should've had her butt over at Lowell Junior High where she belonged. But there she was, strolling hand in hand with some boy with a big Afro, who was wearing black pants and a black leather jacket. Charlesetta, Chantelle's best friend, was with them. She was all hugged up with another boy, who was also wearing black pants and a black leather jacket. It looked like he was trying to wear his hair like the boy with Chantelle, but his was more a fuzzy helmet of naps than an Afro. Maybe that's why he liked Charlesetta; her hair was jacked up too. She caught the ringworm from kissing some nasty boy, and her mama had her daddy cut all of it off and then shave her head. She had to wear a stocking cap for a long time after that. Then again, maybe it was the titties.

Inside my head I was singing a chorus of, "Ooh, um'a tell Mama!" when somebody in our row let out a long, whine of a fart. The snickering started again. Miz Bloom had devastated Deirdre by putting her in Negro Row with the rest of us. Deirdre, determined to earn her way a few rows closer to Miz Bloom, thrust her hand high over her head and waved it back and forth. Miz Bloom looked at her, and nodded. Deirdre stood so her voice would carry when she denounced the sinner. But before Deirdre could say anything, Miz Bloom leaped into the air and screamed.

"What the bloody hell!"

The girls looked around in confusion. The boys hooted and howled with laughter. Darnell was laughing so hard he dropped to the floor, and rolled over onto his back with his legs up in the air, pumping like he was a dying cockroach.

A big, extra gooey, wad of chewed paper clung to Miz Bloom's forehead just above her left eye. She swiped at her face with the inside of her arm, trying to get rid of the spitball without actually touching it. Deirdre bolted to the crafts table, grabbed a handful of paper towels, and vaulted over Darnell—who had by then rolled all the way to the front of the classroom—to minister to Miz Bloom who, out of her mind with panic, kept slapping Deirdre's hands away. But Deirdre stood her ground and did her duty, grabbing the glob and throwing it into the wastepaper can.

Miz Bloom sank down on her chair with her legs splayed out under the desk. She wasn't any good after that, and we had the run of the classroom. Most of the girls colored quietly, but some of the boys formed a group and performed "Hand Jive" at the front of the class. Linda and Melba asked me if they could comb my hair and I said okay. I knew they couldn't stand me, and were nice to me only because of my hair, but I didn't care. They took my braids down and ran their fingers through my hair making "umm, umm" sounds like they were eating something delicious. Nobody tried to leave before the bell rang because we knew we would be hunted down and brought back, probably in chains.

When the bell finally rang, I dashed out to catch up with Chantelle, but when I got where I'd seen her, nobody was there. I felt like a balloon was slowly inflating inside my chest. There was air in there but I couldn't get at it to stop myself from suffocating. I had a real bad feeling about Chantelle and that boy. About everything. But I just couldn't put it into words.

I wished Chantelle and I were best friends the way we used to be, before she started hanging out with Charlesetta and telling her secrets to her instead of me. I could have helped Chantelle figure things out. Maybe I could have saved me and Chantelle from the stupid things we did later on when we both got desperate for completely different reasons.

CHAPTER 4

The river-wide Nimitz Freeway rumbled through West Oakland, separating the part where people lived from the other part that held our elementary school, a whole bunch of factories and warehouses, and trains that hoboes rode. There was no bridge to take you over the Nimitz. You had to go down in a tunnel to get to the other side. When you were in the tunnel, it sounded like you were underwater. It smelled funny, too like old men had been peeing under there and like maybe a rat or two had died. When you stood at one end of the tunnel and looked all the way through to the other end, it seemed like it would take the rest of your life for you to get there, and once you did, you still wouldn't be able to squeeze through the tiny hole of light.

Everybody had to go through the tunnel to get home, and that's where the fights broke out. Somebody would say, "Um gonna kick yo' ass after school!" and you had to go around all day with that soapy feeling in your stomach because you knew they would be waiting for you in the tunnel. Sometimes you could sneak away from school before the bell rang, but the bad kids figured that out, and they were always there waiting for you. If you did manage to get there before them—your heart beating real fast—and you were beginning to think you were going to make it through before they could catch you, and you were right in the middle, almost there, and the light hole was looking bigger, you'd hear the tunnel pick up an extra roar that sounded like a million elephants coming after you, and at that moment, you might as well just sit down where you were and start crying, asking for your mama.

I never walked through the tunnel alone, if I could help it. But I'd spent so much time trying to find Chantelle that I'd missed all of my friends. Now I was going to have to make it through on my own. At first I didn't see anyone, but I was in luck. As I stepped into the mouth of the tunnel I saw three little first graders. I have to admit I was glad to see them, too. A group of babies is almost as good as one full kid. And they were so cute. The two girls wore jumpers, one purple corduroy and the other navy and baby blue plaid. Both wore white tights. The little boy wore boy stuff, navy blue corduroy pants, a navy blue sweater zipped to his neck and heavy-duty brogans.

The little girl in the plaid whispered something to the one in corduroy who nodded and turned to face the little boy. He planted his feet and stood his ground.

"I ain't scared of you," he said.

The little girl answered by raising both hands and shoving him hard in the chest. He did a kind of backward cha-cha-cha, trying hard to stay on his feet, but he landed on his butt anyway.

I ran to them.

"Hey, don't be messing with him," I shouted using my grown folk's voice.

The little girl who had done the shoving teared up. The other one glowered at the boy. He sprung to his feet struggling to look wronged and dusted himself off.

"She colored a picture for her grandmama who's in the hospital and he took it," the little girl who had done the whispering said.

I looked at the other little girl. Tears were streaming down her face now.

"It was pretty . . ." was all she could get out.

I turned to the boy.

"They lying," he said.

"He stuck it in the back of his pants."

He motioned to her with his cocked fist.

"Give it back to her," I said.

He danced from one foot to the other. Then a crooked little smile crawled across his face, and he took off running. When he was far enough to be out of reach but still in shouting distance, he stopped and turned around.

"Hey, you big fat ugly girl. You can't be bossing me around. Who do you think you are? Oh, I know. I heard about you. You the one be doing the nasty with the Sheik."

Bad-assed li'l boy!

I thought about catching him, and bopping him upside the head, but I let that thought go and turned back to the girls. They didn't live far, so I walked them home. On my way back I was trying to make up my mind if I would tell on Chantelle. Regardless what Chantelle thinks, I don't tell *everything*. I wasn't paying much attention to what was happening around me. At some point, I can't really say when, I started hearing sirens, lots of them, lots more than usual. I looked around, and for the first time, I noticed all the kids who had been playing outside had disappeared. When I got to Eighth Street I found the police had it blocked off. They weren't letting anybody go through, even if you lived there. I saw an old man leaning against a street pole, wiping his eyes with the back of his hand. I asked him what had happened.

"They done shot another boy," the old man said. "Killed him dead." He shook his head and pounded the pole with his fist.

"Them police," he said, "Lord, them police."

"How old was he?"

"Twelve," the old man said. "Pauline Howard's li'l boy. This'a kill her for sure."

One year older than me.

I glanced over my shoulder. I felt uneasy like I was smack dab in the middle of a giant bull's-eye. I started humming. I needed to pee. I had to get to someplace safe. I took off running. I had to remind myself to breathe.

Breathe in and out, Bernadine. Breathe in. Breathe out.

I was running as hard as I could but it didn't seem like I was making any progress. It felt like I was wearing boxing gloves on my feet. I was still fighting for breath when I burst through our front door. I stopped short—Mama was standing in the middle of the floor, wearing her coat, hat, and one glove. She was breathing hard like she had run all the way home, too. Her eyes looked strange, kind of crazy. They latched on to my face, darting from my eyes to my mouth and back again like she was looking for clues in some strange game I never heard of.

"Where's Chantelle?"

Before I could breathe in enough air to answer she flung the question at me again. "Where is your sister?"

I wanted to answer. I really did. I tried to answer. But my mouth wouldn't work. Every time I tried to speak, the thought that they were shooting kids welled up inside me and sucked my breath away. I stood there shaking my head, trying to catch my breath, trying to tell Mama that Chantelle was okay, but I just couldn't get it out. Mama's voice was like a siren made out of knives. *Where? Where? Where?* I jammed my hands over my ears. Mama grabbed me by the wrists and snatched my hands away. Her face was inches from mine. It was shiny with sweat, and her breath was hot enough to sting. "Where is your sister?" I forced out one word: "School." "School," I repeated. "I saw her at school."

Mama let go of my wrists, stumbled backward a few steps, and dropped down on the couch. I could see exhaustion smudged under her eyes.

"You mean you ran off and left your own sister?"

I was back to shaking my head.

"What have I told you? You're sisters. You look out for one

29

another. You protect one another. You don't just run off. Lord!"

"I saw her out of the window. She was gone by the time the bell rang."

Mama took my hand and pulled me down on the couch next to her. I wanted to put my head in her lap and scream and cry and kick until my face was hot and smeared with snot and I had a headache. I needed Mama to pat my back, make soothing sounds, and hold the back of her hand to my forehead to make sure I didn't have a fever. I wanted Mama to say, "There, there," and ask me why I was crying so. Then I wanted to tell her how scared I was, that they were killing Negro kids. I wanted to tell her how strange Chantelle started acting once she got titties, I wanted to tell her about the Sheik slapping Jessie Mae. But for some reason I couldn't. So we sat there, me and Mama, like two strangers at a wake for someone neither of us knew.

After a while Mama got up and turned on the radio. We listened a long time before they said anything about the shooting, and when they did, they reported it as a car theft that got messed up.

"A Negro male refused to obey police orders to halt after running from a stolen vehicle during a traffic stop and was shot to death. Oakland police chief called it an unfortunate incident but said the city's law-abiding citizens have nothing to fear."

That was it.

Mama sighed. "Almost makes me glad I have girls."

I didn't say anything to that. What could I say?

Mama said, "Walk with me over to Donna's place."

We went through the kitchen on to the back landing. The landing and stairs were made of metal with holes in them, and each step we took made the landing shake. It sounded like somebody kicking a metal fence. If you stomped real hard it sounded like thunder. Some little kids played all day just stomping on landings. The garbage chute on our landing didn't close right, and the minute we stepped out, the stink of the garbage hit us in the face. Mama stopped and jammed her fist against her stomach. I asked her if she was all right. She held up a hand, and I waited. She kept swallowing like all of a sudden she had too much spit, and then she said she was okay. Somebody upstairs threw something down the chute and we heard it shoot past us, scraping against the walls, all the way down to the dumpster underneath.

Chestnut Court was supposed to be the projects, but it wasn't big enough or bad enough to be real projects. Everybody knew everybody else in Chestnut Court, and somebody's mama was always telling your mama something to get you in trouble. It might have been projects to some people, since projects is a state of mind, as Daddy would say, but it wasn't projects in the way Cypress Court or Harbor Homes was.

It was built around an actual courtyard with wide lawns and a parking lot. Most of the little children played in the courtyard so their mothers or big sisters could watch them from their kitchen windows. We crossed the parking lot, stepping on crooked hopscotches and lopsided foursquare boxes the little kids had drawn. There wasn't a kid in sight. I didn't see any of the guys who liked to hang out in the entryways and harmonize. I also didn't see any of the Grove Street College Boys who liked to get together and talk about politics and stuff.

Miss Donna did hair, but not as good as Mama. Miss Donna was sloppy. She never put anything away after she used it, and her house was full of all kinds of junk and all kinds of people. The worst thing you can say about a Negro woman is that she is lazy—not a hoochie-coochie, not stupid, not mean, but lazy. A lazy woman's kids died of constipation. They choked on fish bones. They were funky and ashy with nappy hair. They got trapped in burning houses full of old newspapers and junk.

Miss Donna wasn't lazy, though. She worked hard doing hair,

writing letters for people, filling out papers so they could get their social security or unemployment, keeping their kids, and minding everybody's business. She was just sloppy.

Round, fat, and the caramel color of Sugar Babies candies, Miss Donna was as pretty as she could be. She looked like she was stuffed with whip cream. She talked loud and laughed a lot. When I was around her, I wanted titties more than ever. People liked her, and they told her all their business and everybody else's too. She knew everything there was to know except how to keep a neat house and how to stop her feet from swelling.

There was usually a game of bid whist or dominoes going at her house with a lot of loud talk and laughter but not that day. "How you all doing?" Mama said to the people in Miss Donna's front room. Their mouths were tight. They shook their heads. They had been talking about the kid the police killed, and at that moment they were too full to speak.

Miss Donna was in the kitchen pressing a little girl's hair and eating barbecue in between times when the hot comb was heating. The girl sat between Miss Donna's knees on an empty plastic twenty-pound chittlin' tub turned upside down. KDIA radio was on and Sam Cooke's "A Change Gonna Come" was playing. The people in the living room started singing along, but the way they sang it made it seem too sad.

"I'm trying to find my fast-ass li'l girl," Mama said.

Miss Donna wiped barbecue sauce on the towel spread across her lap.

"I caught sight of her and Sister Calley's baby boy when I was over at Pon's Market earlier on. Seemed to me they were headed toward the tunnel. But, maybe you ought'a check over at Bea's house."

Miss Bea's was the one of the few places in Chestnut Court that Mama let Chantelle visit without worry. Everybody knew Miss Bea didn't allow any foolishness in her house. Her motto was "respect my house even if you can't bring yourself to respect me."

Mama turned to me. "Run over to Sister Calley's place and see if Chantelle's there. If she isn't, check with Miss Bea. When you catch up with her, tell her to get her ass on home. Don't you go up into any of those entryways either. You hear me? Just holler up there. Then I want both of you to go home and get started on your homework."

I said "Yes, ma'am" and threaded my way out through the junk to the door.

Why is it when grown people want to get rid of you so they can talk, they send you to do something ridiculous?

Even if Chantelle was at one of those places, she wasn't coming out just because I told her to. That was part of the problem. I was always telling Chantelle what "Mama said." That was why Chantelle and her friends talked about me, called me a fink.

I wasn't worried about finding out what Mama and Miss Donna talked about after I left because Miss Donna's little girls were there. I bet I was the only one who noticed four-year-old Sherry under the kitchen table, patting out cookie dough on the floor and sticking it into her Easy Bake Oven that wasn't even plugged in. Six-year-old Maxine was in the hallway leading to the bedrooms, having a tea party with six or seven little chocolate-colored plastic baby dolls wrapped up like mummies and laid out on their backs with tiny tea cups perched on their stomachs. I hoped she hadn't used toilet water for the tea like the last time. Maxine and Sherry knew more about what was happening around Chestnut Court than Miss Donna ever hoped to know, and they loved to talk as much as their mother did.

CHAPTER 5

"Bernadine, I don't know where your daddy is. Will you please stop asking me every six seconds? He's a grown man. He knows his way home."

Mama sounded all bossy and mama-like, but she still had on her coat, even though we had been home from Miss Donna's for hours. And she was doing the hundred-mile march back and forth across the living room.

It was late, almost midnight and Daddy still wasn't home. Sometimes Daddy and Mama went to parties like on New Year's Eve. But never, in my whole life, had Daddy stayed out this late without Mama.

They were shooting Negro kids. Maybe they were shooting grown men, too.

Mama stopped mid stride, bent down, and snatched the telephone cord from the floor. Chantelle had stretched it all the way across the living room, and down the hall to the bathroom. Mama gave the cord a good jerk. "Chantelle, get off the phone and bring it back in here. Your daddy may be trying to call."

Chantelle brought the phone back to the living room, and Mama resumed her march. The next thing I knew, Mama was in the kitchen defrosting the refrigerator. She shoved a pan of hot water into the freezer compartment to thaw the ice buildup. While the ice was slowly loosening, she rearranged all the kitchen cabinets, and mopped the floor. When I asked her why she was doing all that, so late at night, she said, "A busy woman keeps busy."

Chantelle and I spent most of the night on our knees on the sofa, staring out the living room window, trying to make Daddy appear through the combined force of both our wills.

Daddy finally dragged through the front door a little after one. He just shook his head when Mama asked him where he had been. He didn't shake it like he was refusing to tell her. It was more like he was too full to speak. We waited.

"I had to go see the place where they killed that boy. I had to see it for myself."

Daddy said all kinds of people—men, boys, women, and even old ladies—came to see the place where the police killed the boy. They stood there without saying a word, staring at the dried blood on the sidewalk. They probably would have stood there all night bearing silent witness if the city hadn't sent a fire truck to wash away the blood.

The next day was a school day for us and a work day for Mama and Daddy, but nobody went anywhere. Mama didn't tell us we could stay home from school but she didn't say anything when we didn't go. We felt emptied, hollowed out. Yet, we were jittery as a fly trapped between a screen and windowpane.

Daddy found out there was going to be a rally for the dead boy later that evening, and said he was going.

"Don't go, Alex," mama said. She paused a moment and added, "Please."

"I got to."

Mama and Daddy didn't say anything for a long time, then they started pacing. Both stuck to what seemed like previously negotiated routes. Daddy went from the bedroom to the living room where he would pause, peek out the living room window, turn around, and do it over again. Mama's route took her from the kitchen to the living room, where she would stop, place her hands on her hips, and turn around in a circle like she was looking for something she'd lost but couldn't remember what it was. Then she would go back to the kitchen, and do it all over again. They had quick, sharp little arguments under their breaths when their paths intersected. I was on the sofa struggling to hem a skirt the way Mama had shown me. I wasn't supposed to be off in her and Daddy's business, but when Mama said, "Baby, please don't go," I slapped my hands over my mouth to keep from giggling. I couldn't help it. It made me feel funny to hear Mama talking to Daddy all mushy like that.

"What if the police start beating people? What if they start shooting?"

Daddy said, "What if they do? They not the only ones can carry a piece."

"Baby, please don't take—," Mama glanced at me. The thimble conveniently popped off my thumb, and I dived to the floor to get it. I stayed down there for a while. Out of sight, out of mind—that's my motto.

Mama lowered her voice. "Alex, don't take that gun out of here."

"First you don't want me to go 'cause the police may be knocking heads, but if I do go you want me to get naked."

Daddy's voice got squeaky when he was mad, and he was really squeaking now.

"I'm a man, Vondra. I gotta stand for something. This isn't Mississippi, but it might as well be. They can't keep shooting babies, beating on anybody they want to, while we stand around with our fingers up our behinds waiting for Martin Luther King or somebody to come save us."

"What if something happens to you? I can't raise these children by myself."

"So that's what it is? You need somebody to help you raise your children?"

Mama dropped her head. "They're your children too Alex, all of them. You know that." Her voice was softer than I had ever heard it.

"Really? Not from what you said the other day when you told me to stop interfering with you and *your* girls. Maybe you should look up Josh. I hear he's real big on not interfering."

Mama didn't say another word as Daddy left to go to the rally for the dead boy.

I reclaimed my place on the couch. Mama marched another hundred miles from the kitchen to the living room and back again.

"What's wrong, Mama?"

"You know good and well what's wrong, Bernadine. Your fool-ass daddy's out there trying to prove he's a man."

I meant a different what's wrong. I meant, why had she turned on the water so I wouldn't hear her throwing up in the kitchen sink? I meant, was she sick? You see, I was still a kid and I didn't know what all that throwing up meant.

Somebody knocked on the front door. I got up to answer it but Chantelle shot out of the bedroom and elbowed me out of the way singing, "I'll get it!"

It was Charlesetta.

"Good evening, Miss Vondra. How y'all doing?"

She sounded so phony.

Mama said, "Charlesetta, what are you doing running around by yourself at night? You know it's not safe."

"I just wanted to give this to Chantelle." Charlesetta handed something in a paper sack to Chantelle.

"You've given it to her; now take your behind on home. And tell Janice I said hello."

"Yes, ma'am. Bye, Miss Vondra. Bye, Chantelle. Bye, Bernadine."

Charlesetta and Chantelle waved to one another like one of them was going on a long trip. I felt like flipping off Charlesetta's phony ass, but I didn't because Mama was looking. But, I closed the door hard enough for Charlesetta to get the message.

Mama shook her head. "Janice ought to look after that child better than she does"

Chantelle reached into the sack and pulled out a big blue box of Kotex sanitary napkins. I sat there behind my blank face trying to figure out what she needed Kotex for. She couldn't be on her period—our bedroom wasn't all clouded with funk. Mama wouldn't let Chantelle take a bath when she was flowing, and Chantelle never put enough talcum powder where she really needed it.

Mama glanced at the calendar on the wall by the kitchen before asking, "What are you doing going outside of the house and begging people for pads? I thought I raised you better than that. When will you learn it's not becoming to go around talking under your clothes?"

Chantelle rolled her eyes and said, "Oh, Mama." Then she went straight to the bathroom and ran the water a long time before going back to the bedroom. The run-the-water trick was getting old. I could tell she was in there throwing up again.

I said, "You and Chantelle must be coming down with something, the way you both been throwing up."

Mama turned to me with her hands on her hips. "What are you talking about?"

"I sure hope I don't catch it, too."

She backhanded me. I didn't see it coming, but I swear I saw stars afterward. A whuppin is one thing, but a surprise attack is wrong. Purely wrong. And I felt like telling her so, but all I said was, "What did I do?" I knew I sounded like a baby, and I probably looked like one, too all teary eyed and everything, looking up at her from the floor.

Mama didn't answer. She just stood there looking down at me. She had a funny look on her face like she had forgotten something or maybe remembered something she didn't know she'd forgotten. She squatted down. I thought she was going to hit me again, and I tried to scrabble out of her way. But she didn't hit me. She helped me up, and when I was on my feet she wouldn't let go of me.

She hugged me.

"I'm so sorry, Sugar," she said to the top of my head. She rested her chin there and rocked me a little.

"It's okay, Mama," I said. "It's okay." I used a soft voice, and I patted her back. Mama was making a funny sound like she had a cold and her nose was stopped up and she couldn't breathe right. We stood like that for a long time, hugging one another, rocking back and forth. Then Mama went to the bathroom. She walked in, turned around and walked back out.

"Chantelle, get your nasty ass back in here!" The old mama was back.

Chantelle opened the bedroom door and stuck her head out. "What?"

"Wrap that bloody thing up in some newspaper and go drop it down the chute. You're not the only one who lives here."

Chantelle said, "Sorry," all soft and sweet like she really meant it.

"And you and Charlesetta aren't fooling anybody."

Chantelle answered, "What? What?" like she was an owl that had forgotten how to say "who."

Mama sighed. Then she said, "I got too much on my mind right now to deal with this. Trust me, though, we will deal with it, and it'll be soon." Then she went back to her hundred mile march.

Chantelle cleaned up her mess and went back to the bedroom. I got a book, and settled down on the couch. Reading something, anything, usually relaxed me, soothed me, and transported me away from my troubles. But, not that night. I kept reading the same sentence over and over. Frustrated, I slammed the book shut. I looked over at Mama. She had stopped midstride and was staring up at the ceiling. Upstairs noises. They had started again. First, there were sounds of scuffling. Then I heard the Sheik speaking low, saying something I couldn't understand. He didn't sound angry, but I could hear Jessie crying. It

39

was the most pitiful sound I have ever heard. Imagine if you took a little kid way out deep into the jungle in the middle of the night where there were lions and tigers and giant gorillas and big ol' snakes, and you left that little kid out there all by herself. Imagine how she would cry. Jessie Mae was crying like that. Every once in a while I could hear Lee Ann say, "Come on, Willie, leave the girl alone."

Things upstairs got worse. I know what a slap sounds like. I know what it sounds like when somebody throws you against a wall. I have a pretty good idea what it sounds like to be dragged across a room. Jessie was screaming now, and I was scared. I sure wished Daddy were here.

Frozen into a pillar of salt, Mama stood where she was, her head back, and her eyes fixed on the ceiling.

"Mama . . .?"

She waved me silent.

"He's after that child again," she muttered more to herself than to me. "Bring me the phone."

I was relieved. Mama was going to call the police. Let them beat the Sheik upside the head, and take him to jail. But Mama didn't call the police. She called Miss Donna instead.

When it got real quite upstairs, Mama turned the radio on loud.

The radio blared all night.

CHAPTER 6

I stumbled out of my room the next morning and there was Mama sitting at the table, wearing the same clothes she had worn the night before.

"Daddy here?"

Mama shook her head. For a teeny li'l minute it looked like she was going to cry. I don't know why that scared me so much. I guess nobody wants to see her mama cry. I'd seen Mama cuss people out—get all up in their face—but I'd never seen her cry. I preferred a cussing Mama to a pitiful one any day. Mama held herself still for a second. Then the old look came back, the old Mama. It was weird how she did that.

"Get your sister up," she said. "I don't want anybody to be late today."

I was a mess. The thought of having to walk even within ten blocks of the spot where the police killed that kid made my stomach churn. Daddy wasn't home, and I was scared something bad had happened to him. And for reasons that I couldn't explain at the time, I was worried about Mama.

"I don't want to go to school."

Mama cocked an eye at me.

I quickly added, "I don't feel good. I'm sick."

Pushing herself up from the table, Mama went to the kitchen. She didn't have to say a word, I knew she was going to make some of that nasty tea she always gave us when were sick, no matter what we had. Mumps, chicken pox, run over by a truck—the first thing she gave us was that tea.

"Go get back in bed," she said.

"Chantelle snores. Can I get on the couch?"

Mama nodded. I tried to keep from running to the bedroom to get my blanket and pillow. When I got back, Mama had the cod liver oil in one hand and a big ol' spoon in the other. The hairs stood up on my arms—*not the fish juice!* But I didn't say anything. I would have taken a whole bottle of fish juice and drank a gallon of her tea if that was what it took for me stay home where it was safe and wait for Daddy.

Chantelle didn't bother lying about being sick. She just stayed in the bed, timing her trips to the bathroom for when Mama was in the kitchen. Around nine, Mama started calling people. Nobody knew anything about where Daddy was. Miss Donna said she heard he got arrested when the police broke up the rally. Mama called the police station but they wouldn't tell her anything. She hung up the phone and started doing the hundred mile march.

She had marched for a while, when she stopped abruptly, and turned to stare at me. "I thought you were so sick," she said.

I said, "What?"

Mama just stared at me until I dropped back down on the couch. I didn't know when I'd joined her in the hundred mile march. It just snuck up on me. I wanted to say, "He's my daddy, and I'm worried, too." But I didn't.

After a while, Mama went to her room and came back with her coat and purse. I asked her where she was going, and she said she couldn't just sit and wait; she was going to go find Daddy. But the Grove Street College Boys saved her from having to do that.

We heard somebody fumbling at the door like somebody had a key that didn't fit. Mama snatched it open, and there stood Daddy and about six of the Grove Street College Boys. Daddy had two black eyes and a bloody rag tied around his head. Mama screamed, grabbed

Daddy, and didn't let go of him for the longest time. Then she led him to the couch where he sat down with a lot of care.

Grove Street College Boys took up just about the entire room. They all had Afros. Most of them wore black leather jackets. The one with the nicest jacket and a head of hair so round and perfectly shaped that I wanted to cup it my hands as though it were a dandelion, was Sister Calley's boy. I realized he was the one I'd seen at my school with Chantelle. The one in the dashiki, Charles Jefferson—who had started calling himself Ashanti or something like that—was the one who had been all hugged up with Charlesetta. Tim Morris, Melvin Blank, Michael Giles, Herman Duke—they all had fancy new African names that I couldn't remember.

Chantelle used to sneak out of the house at night to go to their parties. She said they played some bad music but nobody wanted to dance. All they did was sit around in the kitchen and talk about helping the community and stuff like that. That seemed to be what they had in common—they went to Grove Street College and they liked to talk. I heard a couple of them could really rap, especially Brother Calley.

I don't know when she came in, but the next thing I knew Chantelle, decked out in full Makeba, was standing next to Brother Calley. She wore so many head wraps and big pieces of wooden jewelry that I was surprised she made it out of our room without toppling over.

One of the Grove Street College Boys said, "Aasalaamu alaikum, my sister."

Chantelle replied, "Wa-Alaikum Assalam, my brother."

Mama said, "I thought you were so sick."

Chantelle bowed her head and smiled like she was so grown and Mama was way out of line to mention her slight indisposition in front of company.

The light in Mama's eyes changed.

"Somebody better get her *lay-kim-salami* back to that room."

Chantelle pivoted toward the hallway like a soldier and for a minute I thought she was finally going to topple. Brother Calley grabbed her elbow to steady her. Chantelle looked over her shoulder to thank him, but got snared in Mama's glare. Mama didn't say another word. She didn't have to. Chantelle left in as much of a hurry as she could manage, wrapped up like she was in all that African fabric.

Mama stared at Brother Calley but he pretended not to notice. She turned back to Daddy and kneeled down in front of him. She cupped his chin in her hand, "Alex, you alright?"

"I'm fine, baby."

Mama lifted the bloody rag and peeked under it. When she saw Daddy brains weren't dripping out, the old mama came roaring back. She stood up and jammed her hands on her hips.

"I told you not to take your ass out there."

"Pardon me, Sister Mattocks. I know you were worried, and I respect your concern for your man's well-being, but he is just that—a man. And a man doesn't stand idle while the police brutalizes his community."

This came from Brother Calley.

Mama's eyes were two machine guns, their sights locked on to poor Brother Calley.

"Child, you have more nerve than a brass ass monkey. You drag my husband home all beat up and bloody, and you gone stand there in my house and tell me—"

Daddy said, "Vondra."

"What?" Mama snapped like he was me or Chantelle, and she was annoyed for being interrupted.

"Be quiet."

Daddy didn't raise his voice. He didn't cuss or anything, but everybody knew he meant business, including Mama. He got up from the couch, refusing to let anybody help him. Then he did the soul-shake with each Grove Street College Boy, and thanked them for coming to his defense when "the police was beating the shit" out of him. They chuckled, and called each other brother, and talked about the Second Amendment, and how they had the right to carry a piece and protect their communities from oppression and police brutality. Then there was another round of soul-shakes and Grove Street College Boys left.

Mama and Daddy sat there looking at each other. Daddy reached out and placed his hand on Mama's stomach. "How's my baby?" he said. Mama placed her hand over his, but she didn't answer. After a while she said Daddy needed to get out of his bloody clothes, and they went to their bedroom. Mama came out and started a bath for Daddy.

I was glad Daddy was back home. I wanted to hug him too, and tell him about all the things that happened the day before, tell him how scared I had been. But Mama was hogging him, as usual. When Daddy got in the tub, she just had to go in there to wash his back. They were giggling and carrying on. It was so disgusting. Then they went to the bedroom, locked the door, and turned on some music. No more Sam Cooke. This time it was Marvin Gaye—"Let's Get It On." They didn't need any encouragement. I got out the Hoover and started vacuuming.

Dressed in regular clothes, Chantelle came out of the bedroom and plopped down on the couch. Cupping her hands to her mouth, she pretended to shout, "Turn that thing off." When I did, she said, "Mama and Daddy are probably in there doing it."

"So what. You better be careful Mama doesn't hear you talking her business."

Chantelle made a sound in her throat to show she didn't give a care. "They ought'a be worried about somebody hearing their old asses in there trying to get down."

"You always gotta talk nasty." I turned the vacuum back on and then off again. "What'd you say?" I asked

"I said, I did it. Once."

"Nah uh, you didn't. Stop lying."

"I'm not lying. Don't tell anybody. Okay? You the only person who knows."

"What about the nasty boy you did it with? Doesn't he know?

She punched me. "Stop fooling around. This is serious. I might have to go away for a while."

"Why?"

"Something I have to take care of. I might even join the movement."

"What movement are you talking about?"

"You know—The movement!"

"The one with Martin Luther King?"

"Not that one . . ."

"The one with Rocky and Bullwinkle?"

"Ha, ha. You so funny I forgot to laugh."

Where is it?"

"Away!"

"Chantelle, not only do you not know *where* the movement is, you have absolutely no idea *what* it is, either."

"Shows what you know."

"Okay, what bus do you take to get there then?"

She punched me again, though this time her heart really wasn't in it.

"Okay, don't tell me. But I'm gonna tell Mama that you did it."

"No you ain't. 'Cause if you do, she's gonna whup me—and then she gonna whup you, just in case you thinking about doing it, too."

I stood there with my mouth open, wondering is this a *paradox*, or maybe a *conundrum*. No, I finally decided, it's a *dilemma*.

Chantelle said, "Close your mouth; you're attracting flies."

"Listen here, Chantelle. You better stop messing around with boys before you end up pregnant."

Chantelle fell over laughing. She laughed so hard tears ran down her face. The next thing I knew she was curled up on the couch boohooing. I sat down next to her. I touched her foot. She said, "You are so lame." Then she jumped up and ran back to the bedroom, slamming the door and locking it.

CHAPTER 7

I was so sick of people doing it and talking about doing it. I went back to my vacuuming. When I finished, I put a new bag in the vacuum, and went outside to the garbage chute to dump the old one. As I pulled open the metal door and stuffed the bag into the opening, a voice with garbage breath and a tinny echo said, "What do you think will happen if I jump down this here chute?"

I leaned in as far as I dared and asked, "Jessie Mae?"

"Nope."

"What's your name then?"

"Dog Shit."

"Jessie Mae quit fooling. That's you."

"Nope. Dog Shit. Thinking 'bout changing it to Hog Shit."

I let the metal door slam shut and crept halfway up the stairs. "Why you saying bad things about yourself?"

She didn't answer.

Mama would kill me if she ever found out I went anywhere near the third floor. But Jessie Mae never said a word to anybody, and now she was talking to me, and what she was saying was crazy. Deep down inside, I knew she needed somebody to help her, not that I thought I would be the one. I was thinking maybe I could get her to come downstairs and Mama would help her.

"Jessie Mae," I whispered, "I'm coming up."

The top of the stairs was as far as I got. The Sheik had fixed up some kind of wire thing that turned the third floor landing into a giant cage. You could come out to the landing from their apartment to get to the garbage chute, but you couldn't go down the stairs. Jessie Mae was sitting on the naked concrete landing, leaning back against the garbage chute. She had on a dress, but no socks, no shoes, no sweater. She was so skinny she probably could have fit in the garbage chute.

I said, "Hi."

She turned to look at me, then turned back to staring at her toes.

I said, "My name's Bernadine."

She said, "I know your name."

I said, "Why you call yourself out of your name?"

Jessie Mae acted like I hadn't said anything. She started talking, though I don't think she was talking to me. She said, "My granny's name is Alice Louise Bing. She lives at 5957 Signal Road, Bessemer, Mississippi. She used to make all my school clothes. She can make the dresses for an entire wedding in four days. Her mama's name was Queen Ester Bowler; when she was young she could pick more cotton than any man ever. Her mama's name was Ti Lilly. She was one hundred percent Indian. Cherokee. She lived to be 102 years old. She could cure snakebite. Did it all the time. I have three aunties: Auntie Alma, Auntie Belinda, and Auntie Gertie. They are real smart. They are real pretty. Auntie Gertie taught me how to do the Slauson Shuffle. Auntie Alma is a preacher and has her own church. Auntie Belinda can sing better than Tammi Terrell. I have goo-gobs of little cousins: Manboy, Bootsie, Tansy, Jojo, Michael John, Mackie and Jackie—they twins—Jimmy Lee, Artie, Bobby Don, Brenda, and Beebee."

I said, "That's nice." Then I was quiet because I didn't know what else to say. She looked so sad and I didn't want to say anything that might hurt her feelings or something.

I stuck my fingers through the wire and grabbed on like I was the one in a cage. "Can you get out of this thing? Wanna come down to my house?"

"Vaseline might work, or lard."

I said, "Huh? Come again."

"I could grease myself down and just slip through the chute."

"That's three whole stories! You don't want to do that. You'll kill yourself. Break every bone in your body, including your coccyx and your clavicle."

She wasn't listening. She was reciting another long list. This one didn't make any sense at all. The most I could figure out, some of it was stuff you need to make Christmas dinner. She stopped and cocked her head. "They coming back," she said. She got up and went inside.

I stood there, gripping the wire until my fingers hurt. It was a doggone shame the way Jessie Mae was being treated. It was like back in slavery days. Everybody knew she was being mistreated but nobody did anything about it. They marched when that kid got shot by the police. What about Jessie Mae? If the grown folks wouldn't do anything, what chance did a kid stand? That's when it started for me, that feeling that twisted me inside out, that had me doing things I never thought I'd do in a hundred years.

Mama was sitting at the kitchen table drinking a cup of coffee and thumbing through a *Jet* magazine. She had on the fancy silk robe Daddy bought her for Valentine's Day. She looked up when I came in and smiled.

"What's the matter? You seen a hant?"

If you were born down South like Mama and Daddy, you said "hant" instead of ghost. If you were born in California, like me and Chantelle, you never said hant—it sounded too country. Mama liked to tease us even though she knew, good and well, we hated it when she talked country.

I said, "I went to put some garbage down the chute, and I heard Jessie Mae up there talking to herself."

Mama's smile vanished. "Don't let me catch you going up those stairs. You hear me?"

"Yes, ma'am, but she sounded so sad. I think she needs somebody to help her."

"Bernadine—"

"Yes, ma'am."

Mama sighed. "You gotta learn to stay out of grown folks business."

"Where's Daddy?" I asked.

"He's back there in the room, but don't you go bothering him; he's trying to sleep."

It was my turn to sigh.

"I don't see what you got to sigh about. By the way, where is your sister?"

"Isn't she in the room?"

Mama sighed again. I tried not to breathe too deeply so she wouldn't think I was sighing too. I went to me and Chantelle's room and lay on my bed. I got up and stood in front of the mirror over the dresser. I pulled up my blouse and held it under my chin. I grabbed my undershirt from the back and pulled it tight. No titties whatsoever. I flopped down on the bed and tried to think of something happy, something that wasn't disappointing or sad or scary. But all I could think about was Jessie Mae. I kept seeing her pitiful li'l self sitting on that cold concrete right under the garbage chute.

Believe me, that was a sad sight.

CHAPTER 8

I didn't have scarlet fever or a broken leg with the bone sticking out, so Mama made me go to school the next day. Nobody at school said anything about the kid the police killed. It was as though some things just shouldn't be rolled across the tongue and spit out by the human mouth. We reacted to the killing the way grown folks do to cancer—it was out there, nobody knew why you got it, but some people did, and it could strike anybody at any time for no reason at all. And the worst part was not even your mama, your daddy, and all your uncles and aunties put together couldn't save you.

We worked hard, exhausted ourselves, trying not to think about the kid the police killed and how sad his mama and daddy was, and how that kid would never ever ask for anything for Christmas again.

When we relaxed long enough to forget we were Negroes and remember we were kids, sometimes a *thought* about the kid the police killed would escape from where we locked it in the back room of our minds, and it would dash across our minds. That was enough to make our tongues feel too big for our mouths, to make our throats feel like we'd swallowed an ice cube as big as a kickball.

Once when Mama sent me to get some insurance papers from her room, I found an old *Jet* magazine she was keeping for some reason. It had a story in it about a Negro kid named Emmett Till, and it told how some white folks down South teamed up and murdered him. There were pictures of this kid in his coffin with his head all swollen up and lopsided, looking ill-treated and almost inhuman. The shock of seeing what some people would do to a kid made me so dizzy I almost fell down. For a second I didn't know where I was. Mama came looking for me and found me standing, unmoving, holding that magazine in my hand. Thinking about the kid the police killed made me feel like that all over again.

I used to think that what happened to Emmett Till was the worst thing that could happen to a Negro child, but that was before they killed those little girls at church, before they started shooting kids in Oakland, and before I met Jessie Mae.

We kids were weighted down with things we were afraid to think about, questions we didn't ask, fears we never put into words. They killed a white man who was the president. Our daddies weren't white, and they would never be president, and we knew they were no safer than the man who had been both. No matter how large our daddies loomed in the doorway when they came home from work, we knew. We didn't dare say any of this out loud because if our daddies weren't safe then they couldn't keep us safe, and we were embarrassed for them and terrified for ourselves.

So we kept quiet, held this terrible knowledge deep inside ourselves, afraid that if we put it into words, we would lose our ever-loving minds. We would leap from our desks in the very back of the classroom and punch Miz Bloom in her big fat nose. We would cuss out the principal, Ol' Shakin' Zimmerman. We would throw rocks at the Cafeteria Lady. Then we would run off, hop a train, and join the hoboes.

That evening, I was in the bedroom reading when the phone rang. I knew it wasn't for me, so I didn't bother getting up to answer it. Mama picked it up in the living room, then whisper-screamed, "Lord, have mercy! Where?" I went to see what had happened.

Mama gave me the saddest look and said, "Bernadine, don't you ever do anything like this to me."

I said, "What?"

Mama said, "Keep your voice down. I don't want Alex all in this."

I whispered, "What?"

Mama turned away without answering. She was struggling with her coat, trying to put it on with one of the sleeves tucked inside itself.

I said, "Here, Mama, let me help."

"No, you run over to Bea's house, right quick, and I'll follow you. They say that fool child of mine is over there with Charlesetta trying to get up her nerve to jump off the second floor landing."

Chantelle was all lumped up on the ground with a bunch of little kids crowding around. I took off running to her. Kneeling next to my sister and looking nervous, Charlesetta was muttering, "Come on, girl, you better get up." I fell to my knees almost before I stopped running. I shoved Charlesetta out of my way with both hands. She hadn't seen me coming, and I caught her off balance and off guard. She fell over hard, scraping her elbow, and came up cussing, ready to fight. I gave her a look—that's what they say, I don't remember—I gave her a look that stopped her dead.

Chantelle was a whimpering mess. Her knees and the palms of her hands were all scraped up and bloody and one foot was twisted funny. I brushed her hair out of her eyes and whispered, "Chantelle, why you so stupid?" She tried to smile. I used the back of my hand to wipe away her tears, ignoring mine. All of a sudden Charlesetta took off running. The next thing I knew Mama was there next to me breathing hard and praying out loud. I think she was asking the Lord the same thing I had just asked Chantelle. Mama shoved her purse at me, and then she stooped down and scooped up Chantelle just like she was a baby.

"Listen to me, you fool-ass girl. You're going to have this child."

And that's when I knew. It was hard for me to admit, even to myself, that I'd missed all the clues, and got Chantelle's hints all wrong.

I dug the car keys out of Mama's purse, followed them to the car and helped Mama load Chantelle into the back seat.

I waved goodbye as they sped off. I couldn't think of anything else to do.

Mama and Chantelle got home around nine that night. Mama walked in first without bothering to hold the door for Chantelle who stood there with one ankle bandaged, looking like Mama had tied a string to her and dragged her all the way home. Daddy grabbed the door before it could slam in her face. He put his arm around Chantelle's shoulders and helped her through the door. "How you doing, baby girl?"

Chantelle grimaced and moaned a little.

"That's alright, Peaches. Every thing's gonna be alright, you hear. Where you want Daddy to take you—to the couch, to your room?"

Chantelle wanted to go to our room. Daddy helped her hobble there.

Mama dropped down on the couch without bothering to take off her coat. Daddy came and stood over her.

"Woman, what's the matter with you? You see the girl hurt. Why you want to slam the door in her face like that?"

"Alex, please don't start. I'm the one been sitting up at Highland all day and half the night."

"You didn't have to be. The girl has a daddy, you have a husband. Why didn't you let me know the child was hurt?"

"One day you'll thank me."

"Thank you?" Daddy was shouting, which was about as rare as a turtle with two heads and three tails.

"I didn't want you to have to be the one to have some white doctor get up in your face and tell you that your *baby girl* went out and got herself knocked-up."

55

Daddy's eyes went all shiny. He said, "What?"

"That's right," Mama said. "She has sneaked around with some pissy-assed li'l boy and now she's pregnant. Her and Charlesetta cooked up all kinds of little schemes to get rid of it, including jumping off the second-floor landing. You think I'm too harsh with the girls. Now, you see why I try so hard to keep them under control. This is exactly what I was afraid of. Thirteen years old."

Daddy said, "Who's the boy?"

"She hasn't gotten around telling me, just yet."

Daddy fell into the hundred-mile march. After about seven hundred and sixty-two miles he stopped in front of Mama and squatted down so they were eye to eye. He placed his palms on Mama's stomach. Mama covered his hands with hers.

"Now, like I told you before, Vondra, I don't believe in getting rid of babies . . ."

"She's going to have the baby, Alex. Make no mistake about it. I made it very clear to her that she's got to stop this foolishness trying to get rid of it."

"And you told her we would help her raise the child?"

Mama hesitated for a moment. "Yes, I told her that."

"And us, Vonda, what about us?"

Mama held up her hand like she was a traffic cop and said, just one word, "Alex."

That "Alex" seemed to say a thousand things and none of them had a question mark at the end.

Mama and Daddy argued back and forth without uttering a word. Their eyes did all the talking. Daddy was almost ten years older than Mama, but her eyes were harder than his and, as usual, he lost. He stood up and said, "I'm telling you, Vondra." Then he stomped off to their bedroom and slammed the door. But Daddy couldn't stay gone long. After a while he came back and sat down on the couch next to

Mama, put his arm around her shoulders, and hugged her to him.

CHAPTER 9

A few days later, I got home from school and found Mama on the couch.

"I think I have a fever," she said. "Get me some BC Powder will you baby."

I went to the bathroom and got it for her. On my way to the kitchen for some water, the phone rang. Chantelle limped to the bedroom doorway like the bell was her summons. Mama told her to go back to bed and asked me to get it.

It was Miss Donna. I said, "Mama's not feeling too good right now. I was just getting ready to give her some BC powder. Want me to—"

Miss Donna started screaming at me. I couldn't understand everything she said because I had to hold the phone away from my ear to keep her from busting my eardrum—she was screaming just that loud.

Mama raised up on an elbow. "What is it, Bernadine?"

"It's Miss Donna. She's saying something about aspirin—something about bleeding."

Mama lay back down. "Give me the phone."

By the time I got the cord untangled and dragged the phone over to Mama, Miss Donna had hung up. It seemed like a couple of seconds later she was hammering on the front door. I opened it and Miss Donna rushed in and snatched the glass of water I had given Mama, snatched it right out of her hand.

"Vondra, what you trying to do, kill yourself? No aspirin. I told you."

"I'm just taking a little BC Powder."

"That's aspirin, woman!"

Mama said, "Oh."

"What you doing out here on the couch? You went to work, didn't you? Why didn't you stay home for just one day?"

Mama said, "Couldn't—too many mouths to feed."

"Come on girl, get up. Let me help you to your bed." Miss Donna put her arm under Mama's and dragged her upright, slapping my hand away when I tried to help.

"Mama, you okay?" I asked, trying hard to control the quaver in my voice.

Miss Donna snapped, "Everything's fine."

But it didn't look like everything was fine. Mama was burning up. She radiated heat. I could feel it from where I was standing. Her face was slick with a landslide of Dixie Peach that had melted off her hair. A muddy puddle of blood marked the spot where she had been lying on the couch. It probably wasn't much blood, but it was enough to choke a scream out of me, and another and another, until I was lost somewhere, trapped by the blood and its woman smell, unable to do anything but scream.

Miss Donna slapped me. It was just like on TV when somebody slaps the screaming white girl and says, "Dammit, Becky, pull yourself together!" Only Miss Donna said, "Shut the fuck up, Bernadine!"

I wasn't the only one scared.

When Daddy got home, he found me and Chantelle wedged into a corner of the couch, as far away from the bloodstain as we could get, clinging to one another like we used to do when we were little. He took one look at us, and dropped his lunch pail and the jacket he carried slung over his shoulder, and bolted to the bedroom. A slew of women crowded the bedroom ministering to Mama. They fanned her, placed cold compresses on her forehead, and spooned crushed ice into her mouth. Daddy stood unmoving in the doorway.

Miss Donna approached him, "Alex . . ." she said, trying to find the right words.

Daddy tightened his hands into fists but kept them at his side.

"Get away from her," he said through gritted teeth. "All of you, get the hell out of my house."

He dropped to his knees at the side of the bed. The women squeezed out of the room, carefully stepping over his legs so as to do no more harm.

Daddy took Mama's face in his hands. He kissed her parched lips. "Vondra, why?"

She closed her eyes like she was too weak to bear the sight of his pain.

"I told you, baby, a man takes care of his family. Why didn't you let me?"

Mama squeezed her eyes tight and shook her head.

"What's one more mouth, Vonnie?"

Mama opened her eyes. "A whole lot," she said. "A whole lot more than you will ever know."

"You didn't have to do this. You didn't have to get rid of our baby."

"Better me . . ."

Some things are too hard to hear. Daddy touched his fingers to her mouth. "Don't say that, baby. Please."

But Mama wanted Daddy to know the terrible truth. She wanted him to know the high price you paid when you were somebody's mama. She wanted him to know how much courage it took to mother a Negro child, how much courage it took to love one, because the world was full of heartbreak from sun up to sun down, from one auction block to another, from the cotton fields of Mississippi to the sidewalks of San Pablo Avenue. She wanted him to know how fearless you had to be. Fear made you falter, made you forget that sometimes you had to slap your own child down or the world would do it for you. *I'd rather kill you than have someone else do it.* Sure, Miss Donna had washed her hands and put a clean bed sheet on the kitchen table, but that table top was no place for a child—no place for Chantelle—and Mama wanted Daddy to know that. She wanted him to know that when you were somebody's mother you would rather take the homemade tonic yourself, wear a steel wool tampon, if you had to. You would do all that and more if it meant your child didn't have to.

She wanted Daddy to know all of that.

"Better me than Chantelle," she said.

But Daddy already knew that and a whole lot more. And what he knew clawed at his heart each and every minute of each and every day. But he kept it to himself because he loved Mama too much to maim her with his knowledge.

"What about me?" he asked Mama. "Don't I have any say?"

Mama didn't answer. She'd said what she had to say, and there was nothing more.

I heard it all, every single word. But Chantelle swears to this very day that Mama whispered little more than a word or two before Daddy bundled her up and rushed off to Highland.

Chantelle cried for a long time after they left—real tears. She cried loud and hard. She cried like Mama was dead, and it was all her fault.

"You think it might have been a boy?" I asked. "You think we could have had us a little brother?"

Chantelle cried even harder.

For three days the nurses briskly ministered to Mama as she drifted toward death. They weren't mean, they just didn't approve of what she had done, and they let her know by their indifferent handling. It was her fault she was there in that condition, and she deserved no

61

sympathy. It was her fault that she was stupid enough, black, and poor enough to let somebody stick something inside her and tear her all up like that. They referred to Daddy as her "boyfriend." They tried to get Mama to tell them who did that to her so they could have them arrested. Mama wouldn't tell on Miss Donna and Daddy didn't either, although he wanted to, and after a while they stopped asking.

They put Mama in the maternity ward where she bled and burned and listened to other women's babies cry. She cried too, but quietly so the nurses wouldn't hear her. They cried—she and the other women who were there for the same reason as Mama, who were there because they were black, white, yellow, brown enough and poor enough to have no way out other than the butchers and amateur butchers. Mama's fever broke on the third day and the bleeding stopped soon after, and they told her she could go home.

"There will be no more babies," the young intern told her. "No more for the rest of your life."

CHAPTER 10

Things only got worse.

It was just a few nights after Mama got home from the hospital. I was asleep when it started but Chantelle told me about it. According to her, the Sheik started in on Jessie Mae, preaching and shouting and quoting scripture. Some of the Bible isn't fit for Sunday school. I know. Chantelle is my sister, and nobody knows the nasty parts of the Bible better than her. She knows the location of all the laying withs, the begats, and seed spillings, and she has shown each and every one of them to me—at least a hundred times.

Chantelle got out of bed, went to Mama and Daddy's room, just as bold as she could be, and told them she couldn't sleep.

"Daddy," she said, "he up there reading the nasty parts of Genesis 19:30 out loud."

According to Chantelle, Daddy shot out of bed like Sputnik. Mama tried to grab him, but all she got was a handful of his pajama shirt. Daddy didn't slow down. Buttons exploded like popcorn and Mama was left clutching the shirt. She climbed out of bed and slung it at Chantelle. "Now, see what you've gone and done."

Meanwhile, King Kong had climbed up the side of our building and was growling and cussing and beating on my window, trying to get in. I woke up with my heart in my throat. I whispered Chantelle's name. She didn't answer. Her bed was empty. I checked the window to see if maybe I hadn't been dreaming after all, and King Kong really had been there, and he had broken the window and snatched my sister. The window wasn't broken. King Kong was just a dream, but the noise was not. Somebody was shouting and cussing and knocking against walls. I heard someone scream. It sounded like Mama. I was out of bed before that scream ended. I followed its tail through the front door, onto the landing, down the stairs, and all the way out to the middle of Chestnut Street.

"You bad, mothafucka. You beat on your woman. You mess with little girls. Come on." Wearing only his pajama bottoms, Daddy was dancing and jabbing like he was Cassius Clay. The Sheik just stood there. Daddy was shorter than the Sheik by a couple of inches and smaller too, but with his muscles glistening under the streetlights, he looked like Hercules to me.

I had never seen Daddy act like that, or heard him talk bad either. Until that night, I didn't know he knew how to cuss. Daddy was the nonviolent, non-cussing one in our family. He worked his crossword puzzles, told silly jokes, and let us get away with stuff. He was . . . daddy-like. Under the streetlights that night he was somebody totally different, and I have to admit, it scared me a little.

The Sheik backed up, trying to keep out of Daddy's reach.

"Jessie Mae?" he sang out in his preacher's voice. "You talking 'bout her? I ain't never touched that poor, wretched cur. Blaspheme! Oh, Blaspheme!"

A crowd had gathered. It was eleven at night, but a fight would draw spectators any time, any day, any place. Lee Ann was standing off to the side, wringing her hands. Every once in a while she would say, "Ya'll quit it," but nobody paid her any mind. I didn't see Jessie Mae.

Later on, after listening to countless retellings of what happened, I found out the Sheik said, "I ain't playing with you, nigger. You better go on."

Daddy said, "Now, why I got to be the nigger?"

The Sheik danced his little preacher jig and sang, "Yass! Your throat be an open grave. Your tongue-agh! It be deceiving."

Daddy said, "I'm tired of this shit," and hauled off and slapped the Sheik hard. People say they thought the Sheik's head was going to spin all the way around like Charlie McCarthy's. Spit sprayed out his mouth and some blood too. He got teary eyed. People in the crowd mouthed a long, "O-o-o-h!" and starting giving one another fives.

The Sheik said, "Hit me again, and um calling the police,"

"You sure you want to do that? Daddy asked. "If I were you, I'd be scared to call the white man here and tell them about how I been messing with somebody's baby."

The Sheik spit in Daddy's face, and the crowd got so excited it almost cheered. Boys hopped up and down to see over the shoulders of grown folk.

Daddy didn't bother to wipe off the spit. He slammed his fists into the Sheik so hard and so fast that people said they didn't even see his hands move. The Sheik dropped to his knees, then to all fours with his head hanging down like the dirty dog that he was. Blood splattered the sidewalk under him.

"Shit, man you see that! Cold cocked the mutha!"

The crowd got quiet, waiting for Daddy to finish off the Sheik. Miss Viola's little boy, Heman, danced around the edge of the crowd, demonstrating how he would do an upper cut and then stomp the Sheik 'til his guts squished out.

Mama forced herself between Daddy and the Sheik. "Don't kill him," she screamed in Daddy's face. "The girls, Alex. Think about the girls!"

Daddy stopped dancing. He shook his hand and blew on his knuckles. "Where my girls at?"

He found Chantelle in the entrance sitting on the stairs with her arms locked around her knees, weeping.

They couldn't find me.

Later on they said they didn't even think about looking upstairs in the Sheik's apartment. That was the last place they expected to find me.

Jessie Mae didn't look up when I came through the open door. She sat on the couch in her slip, her head hanging down, and her arms dangling between her knees. She looked like most of her was gone—there was only a little bit left.

"You betta git out'a here before he catches you," she said, still not looking at me.

"He mess with me, my daddy kick his ass. Come on, I'm gonna help you get away."

She didn't move.

I hadn't given the escape plan much thought. I said, "We're going to my house . . . then to your grandmother's."

"You don't even know my grandmother."

"Alice Louise Bing, 5957 Signal Road, Bessemer, Mississippi."

She finally looked up.

I said, "Put your dress on. Where's your coat?"

"I don't have no coat."

I slipped out of my car coat and held it out to her. "Here, take mine."

She stood up, and I helped her into it.

I scurried about the room looking for her shoes. She just stood there. "Where your shoes, Jessie Mae?"

"I can't leave my mama."

I said, "What?"

"It's too late anyway," she said.

I heard people cappin' on the Sheik, saying things like, "You fight like Miss Lillie and she don't got but one leg." I heard him and Lee Ann stumbling up the stairs, muttering and cussing. "Yeah, better take yo' punk ass on home," came from the crowd.

"You one sorry-assed bitch, you know that? Stood right there and let him sucker punch me. Any other woman would have been by her man's side, throwing punches, but not you."

"I had to keep Vonda from jumping in. You know she fights dirty."

"Ouch, don't go pulling on me like that. Don't you see I got injuries?"

"I'm just trying to help you up the stairs, honey."

"Ouch!"

"Sorry, sorry."

I stood bolted to the floor, holding one of Jessie Mae's saddle oxfords. The way she looked at me let me know she felt sorry for me. She took off my jacket and gave it back. I just stood there motionless like a department store dummy. She shoved me. I move a couple of feet. She shoved me again and kept shoving until I was in the kitchen. I heard the front door open right when Jessie Mae opened the back door and shoved me out onto the landing. She closed the door softly behind me. I sat down on the cold concrete and tried to muffle my weeping.

"Bernie Berry, where you at, baby?"

Daddy was out looking for me, calling me by the baby name he'd given me when I was his "sweet little Bernie Berry." I wanted to answer so bad. I wanted to holler at the top of my voice, "Up here, Daddy. I'm up here." I said nothing, though, because there was no way out of the cage the Sheik had built for one girl but had caught another in, so I kept quiet. I had to clamp my hand over my mouth; I couldn't make a peep.

"Everything's alright now, Bernie Berry. Come on out'a where you hiding and let Daddy take you home."

Daddies must be like elephants—they never forget. I bet nobody else remembered how, when I was little, I used to run off and hide when something scared me.

Somebody was in the kitchen. I heard the refrigerator open and close. I heard water running in the sink. I heard the crystal-cracking sound an ice tray makes when you pull back the lever to pop out the cubes.

"What the hell's taking so long with that damn ice pack?" Now, it sounded like the Sheik was in the kitchen.

"It's coming, baby. There you go." That was Lee Ann, the world's sorriest mother.

"What's that stankin' in here?" The Sheik, again.

"Must be the garbage."

"*Somebody* betta get that shit out'a here!"

I heard the door under the sink being opened and the sound of a paper box being dragged out. I tried to scoot deeper into the landing's shadows but there was nowhere to go. Nowhere to go—that must be how Jessie Mae felt every single day of her life with her sorry mother and the Sheik. What was I thinking not calling out to Daddy when he came looking for me, calling me by my baby name? So what if the Sheik had heard me? What could he have done to me anyway with Daddy looking? Drag me into his apartment? Daddy would have kicked in the door. He would have been all over the Sheik like white on rice. I shouldn't have let Daddy leave without me. He was probably all the way past McClymond's by now, calling me by my baby name, begging me to come out from hiding. And to think, I used to call Chantelle stupid.

I looked around for something I could use as a weapon—a machine gun or a big rock, an anvil even. Anything. But there was nothing, just me, the cold concrete, and the garbage chute with its funky breath. I was so scared I had forgotten to breathe. I was about ready to pass out when the door opened. I got up and bent my stiff body into a kung fu position.

Jessie Mae backed onto the landing, bent over, dragging the garbage box. She pulled the door closed, then turned around. From her expression, I could tell I looked like a fool. Shoot, it's hard to do kung fu with your knees knocking and your socks filling with pee. I collapsed on the concrete in my own mess.

Jessie Mae mouthed, "I'll be back." Then she put on a show of banging open the garbage chute, stuffing the box into it, and banging the chute shut.

When she returned to the kitchen the Sheik said, "Look at the dutiful daughter. I ain't forgot how you started this, hooting and hollering like somebody killing you. You will rue the day, hear me. Rue-the-day." Loud pounding on the front door interrupted the Sheik. I put my hands together and prayed, "Please Lord, let it be the police." Turned out it wasn't the police. It was even better.

"I came to get my child."

It was Mama!

The Sheik said, "You don't have no child up here, and you know it. Alex sent you, didn't he?"

"Alex doesn't know I'm here, and he won't know; you give me my baby."

"I told you woman— Where you going? This my house!"

The voices grew louder. They were in the kitchen.

"You think 'cause you a woman you can walk over me in my own house? You think I won't bust you in your ass?"

It got real quiet when the Sheik said that. I couldn't hear anything. I was beginning to panic until Mama said in a slow, calm voice, "It would please me immensely if you tried." There was another long silence, then the Sheik said, "Go ahead. Look. I told you she ain't up here."

The next thing I knew, Mama had jerked opened the back door. When she saw me all crumpled up on the landing, she whipped around and lunged at the Sheik. Lee Ann threw her body between them. Mama struggled to get something from her pocket. Lee Ann, sensing it was a gun grabbed Mama's wrist. Mama strained against Lee Ann. Then everything clicked over into slow motion. Mama's hand, gripping the gun, slowly rose from her coat pocket. Lee Ann struggled to push it back down. Mama forced her arm up until the gun was in firing position with the Sheik dead in its sight. He took off running. Only there was nowhere to go. He couldn't run out of the front door because folks were still there waiting to see more blood splatter. He couldn't run to either of the bedrooms because then he would be cornered. Lee Ann still held on to Mama's arm, but Mama was going wherever she wanted and dragging Lee Ann along with her. Mama remembered Lee Ann was there and shook her off like she was a bug or something.

I made my way to Mama.

"He didn't touch me, Mama. Honest!"

She elbowed me away.

Pleading with the Lord for help, the Sheik was running around in little circles. I didn't want Mama to shoot him and have to spend the rest of her life in prison, though I sure hoped the Lord was laughing at the Sheik.

"He ain't worth it," Lee Ann whispered to Mama. "Child, he sho' ain't worth it."

I knew my mama, and I could have told Lee Ann it was way beyond too late to start talking reason to her.

Mama went to the corner where the Sheik was cowering behind a bent up floor lamp. That in itself would have been hilarious if it hadn't been for the gun Mama was pointing at him. Lee Ann seemed to give up then, and backed away from Mama.

"He ain't worth it," she repeated a final time.

Mama aimed the gun at the Sheik's head. He covered his face with his hands and screamed. I was screaming now. Mama seemed to rethink her target and pointed it at his privates, instead. Then something happened I will never forget as long as I live, even if I live to be fifty or sixty.

Chantelle wedged herself between Mama and the cowering Sheik. Now the gun was pointing at Chantelle's stomach. Chantelle didn't say a word. She just stood there looking Mama in the eye. Mama's shoulders started to shake, and the next thing I knew she was crying. Chantelle took the gun from her and led us back downstairs.

Chantelle ran a bubble bath, and she and Mama undressed me and hustled me into the tub. They didn't know what to do with my pee-soaked clothes so they shoved them under the water and told me to sit on them. Mama poured a whole lot of her bath salts into the hot water to cover the odor. Then she got down on her knees next to the tub, took my towel, lathered it with the bar of Ivory soap, and started scrubbing my back.

"You love you Daddy, don't you, Bernadine?"

I said I did.

"Then you can't let him know what happened, okay? You can't let him know you were upstairs."

"I won't, Mama."

She grabbed my chin and twisted my face to hers. "Listen, Bernadine, this is serious. If your daddy finds out about tonight, he will kill Willie. You understand? Then your daddy will go to prison, and you'll never see him again. That what you want?"

"No, ma'am."

She stared into my eyes like she was trying to read my fortune. Finally, she said, "Okay then," and went back to scrubbing my back.

"Mama, were you really going to kill—?"

She cut me off. "Never you mind. You just remember your promise."

The phone rang. Chantelle answered it.

"It's Daddy," she yelled. "He was going crazy trying to find

71

Bernadine. I told him she came home. He's on his way back."

Daddy was home a few minutes later, breathing hard like he had run the whole way. Mama had left the bathroom open a crack and I could hear everything. The first thing Daddy said was, "Where's Bernie?"

Mama said, "She's in the tub, baby. She should be done in a little bit."

"She alright?"

"She's fine. A little scared, that's all. She heard you calling her and came home."

"I want to see her."

"She's in the tub . . ."

"That's alright; I'm her daddy. Besides, she ain't got nothing but bee stings anyway."

He came to the bathroom door and knocked. "Baby girl, cover yourself up. Daddy's coming in."

Later on in the night somebody attacked the Sheik's girl cage with wire cutters, hacked it apart, and threw the pieces in the middle of the parking lot. Later on I found out it was Chantelle who told Mama I was upstairs trapped in the Sheik's cage.

When I asked her how she knew I was up there she said, "I smelled your special brand of pee drifting down on the cool winter breeze, mah li'l chickadee."

CHAPTER 11

There had been so many fights overnight that hardly anybody at school mentioned Daddy's, which was just fine with me. Most people were going on and on about the fight Nadine's mama had with Shirley's mama after Shirley threw a rock that hit Nadine in the eye; Shirley said she didn't and her mother believed her.

When folks got home to Chestnut Court from school and work, we found out that the Sheik had been busy. He waited until the mamas, grandmothers, aunties, and big sisters were bustling about getting dinner ready, setting the beans to boil that had soaked all day, thawing the ground beef they'd forgotten to take out of the freezer before they left that morning, or making a big bowl of tuna fish salad. He knew that, from time-to-time, they would glance out their kitchen windows that overlooked the courtyard.

And he chose then to march Jessie Mae and Lee Ann on a slow procession from their apartment to the wash house and back again. We saw the purple pouches that had replaced Lee Ann's eyes, the lips beat big, split, and swollen, the crooked, flattened-out nose. We saw how she moved stiff and wide legged. Jessie Mae was no better, no worse, except, between the two of them, she had the one good eye not swollen completely shut.

We got his message. We got it loud and loud and clear. The next time anybody messed with the Sheik, he was going to make Lee Ann and Jessie Mae pay. He had messed them up so bad, the only way he could outdo that was to kill them. That evening, every woman in Chestnut Court daydreamed about how she could kill the Sheik without her man or the law finding out. Some favored taking a razor

73

and slitting his throat. But that would mean they had to get close to look into his serpent's eyes and smell brimstone on his breath. Miss Viola had a gun for her protection, and she would have been happy to shoot him, but she didn't want to waste a bullet on his sorry ass. Miss Donna threatened to go down there and kick his ass herself, and she certainly could and probably would have done exactly that, except her feet were swollen so bad she couldn't get her shoes on.

That is when I began working on my plan. No lame daydreaming for me. No more trembling in a puddle of my own pee in some cage. It was time somebody did something.

"Daddy, can I have some money?"

I timed it so I caught him just as he was leaving for work, and Mama was in the bathroom running water. Daddy stuck his hand into his pocket.

"Getting ready to do some Christmas shopping, huh? How much you need, Bernie?"

"Thirty-one dollars and fifty-two cents."

"Whoa! When you say money, you mean *mon-neh*, don't you baby? I don't have that kind of change. I give just about every cent I make to your mama for the bills."

I said, "That's okay, Daddy," but I was dying inside. My plan for rescuing Jessie Mae hinged on getting enough money to buy her a one-way ticket back to her grandmother in Mississippi—helping her sneak out of the house, getting her to the Greyhound Bus Station, putting her on the bus, and waving goodbye. Without thirty-one dollars and fifty-two cents, the plan wouldn't work, and Jessie Mae was doomed.

There was no way I could ask Mama for that kind of money. She didn't believe in giving kids money—she worked for what she got and figured we should too. By running errands and hoarding money from my birthday in June, I had saved a little over seven dollars in my penny jar, but that wasn't nearly enough.

There was no one else I could turn to. It was Christmas time and the responsible folks were pulling together their money to get stuff off lay-away. Aunt Barbara was supporting three kids all by herself. I couldn't ask her for money. Uncle Fred had a good job, but five or six girlfriends took up most of his money. I had heard of people selling blood, but I was scared of needles. Besides they probably wouldn't take a kid's blood—it wasn't thick enough or something. I even tried looking in the want ads for a job, and for a minute I considered an ad that screamed: "Girls! Girls! Girls! Dancers needed!" I could outdance anybody, but I figured you needed titties to get one of those jobs, so I kept looking. I found nothing.

My last resort, the seed corn one, the one so dire I had refused even to consider it until then, was to try to leverage what I was getting for Christmas.

"Mama, what you and Daddy getting me for Christmas?" I asked with as much sweetness as I could muster.

"A lump of coal."

"I was kinda hoping for some money . . ."

Mama made a "what you said was so funny I'm not even gonna answer" sound deep in her throat.

"Okay, how about a bike?"

"Where you think you going on a bike?"

"I could go to the store for you. I could go to the library. There're lots of useful and helpful things I could do with a bike."

But I was really thinking if I had a bike maybe Jessie Mae could use it to get away. And if they got me a bike and they gave it to me early . . .

Mama snorted.

"Well, how 'bout some skates, then?"

"We'll see."

I knew what that meant.

Just when I was beginning to think about giving up, I came up with an idea so daring it took my breath away. It was dangerous too, because it involved getting all off into Mama's business and uncovering a secret that nobody thought I knew about. That I had to rely on Chantelle for a critical piece of information, only increased the danger.

Me and Chantelle were on the couch with the TV on down low so Mama wouldn't know we had it on instead of doing our homework.

Out of the blue Chantelle said, "Mama was fourteen when she had me."

"Nuh uh, you lying."

"What does Mama say when you ask how old she is?"

"A lady never tells her age," I mimicked.

I could do Mama real good. I had practiced until I had her voice dead on.

Chantelle gave me five. "You good, girl. I give you that. You ought'a get yourself on the Ed Sullivan Show. It could be you and Topo Gigio. Second thought, just do the math."

I did the math. Something didn't add up.

"So, that would make Mama twenty-eight."

Chantelle nodded. "Mama was fourteen when she had me, so I don't see why she giving me all this static."

"And Mama will be a twenty-eight year old grandmother."

"Maybe that's what's got her trippin'."

"Chantelle, why you doing this?"

"Doing what?"

"You know, trying to act all cool, talking like that—trippin' and static, and stuff like that."

"Aw girl, now you trippin' . . ."

"And why did you let some boy stick his thing in your . . . pussy?"

Chantelle loud-talked me. "Why you whispering, Ber-na-deeeen? You scared to say PUSSY out loud? Huh? Huh?"

I punched her in the shoulder. I didn't care if she was in the "family way." It was either that or slap her in her big fat mouth. We tussled on the couch, trying to giggle in whispers so Mama wouldn't hear us. I got Chantelle in a headlock.

"Now tell me," I said. "Who's the daddy?"

"You think I'm telling you?

I let her go. That hurt, the way she said it with such finality. I was her sister, after all. We used to share everything, keep one another's secrets. "Why not?"

"You'd be scratching at Mama's door before I even got the words out'a my mouth"

"I know who it is—Ol' Bad Richard."

"That baby? Huh!"

"How come you won't tell anybody?"

"'Cause I promised I wouldn't."

"Promised who?"

She opened her mouth to tell me before she caught herself.

"What about Daddy? How come you won't tell him?"

"'Cause he's worse than you."

"He saved your li'l butt. If it hadn't been for him, Mama would'a beat it out of you."

"That doesn't work, and she knows it."

As much as I wanted to know, I was careful not push Chantelle too far. I didn't want her coming up with some sorry lie just to get me off her case. I'd already had enough fractured fairy tales from Miss Donna's little girl, Maxine.

No matter how many times I explained it to her, Maxine just couldn't get the baby-making division of labor straight. "Max," I said, "for the hundredth time, a boy has to be the daddy and a girl has to be the mama. So now you see why Miss Calley can't be having a baby with Chantelle?"

But Maxine was one stubborn child. She folded her little arms across her chest and shook her head, whipping the five hundred barrettes on her five hundred braids until she sounded like Medusa with a handful of castanets.

"Chantelle, tell me something."

"Long as it's not about something I just told you I'm not telling."

"Where does Josh live?"

You would have thought I had heated a pin in an open flame and stuck her with it, the way Chantelle jumped. She flashed those funny-colored eyes at me.

"You better shut up before Mama hears you. Whatever you do, don't let Mama hear you talking about him. I never mentioned him, never said his name, you hear. And don't be talking any of that Josh mess around Daddy."

"Look," I shot back, "I know who Josh is. Okay? You didn't tell me. Okay? I am not a baby. Okay?"

Chantelle said, "Humph" like she was so sophisticated and I wasn't. "Why you need to know where he lives anyway?" she asked.

"I think I have a right—"

"You don't have any rights when comes to Mama's business."

"It's my business—yours too."

"Leave me out of it. I got enough problems as it is."

I persisted. "I have the right to know who my real daddy is."

Chantelle looked at me like I was something weird. Her eyes watered, her shoulders started to shake, and then she let out a whoop so loud I nearly peed myself. She laughed a good five minutes. I asked her what was so funny.

"And you think you so smart," was all she would say.

I hate it when people laugh at me, especially Chantelle. For a teeny minute I considered forgetting the whole Josh thing. But Jessie Mae had a hold on me, and she wouldn't let go. Every night she stalked my dreams, paralyzing me, holding me down until I screamed myself awake. I was afraid to sleep. Mama tried all kinds of teas and tonics on me. Nothing worked.

"Maybe, its colic," Daddy suggested one night after my screams had turned to howls and everyone was up trying to figure out what was wrong on with me.

Mama laughed. "Half-grown kids don't get the colic." She laughed some more. She kept laughing. She laughed until her pink sponge hair curlers littered the floor. She laughed until I was scared that she would never stop. She laughed until big fat tears rolled down her cheeks. She laughed until she started to sob and Daddy wrapped her in his arms.

Desperation, pure and simple, was driving me to Josh. Chantelle might not have been talking, but I had a source who probably knew his whereabouts, and loved to talk—Miss Donna. One afternoon I sneaked over to Miss Donna's house, and this is what I learned about Big Josh after talking to her for only ten minutes: He was a big, good-looking man with hazel colored eyes; he weighed nearly three hundred pounds, and stood well over six feet; everybody liked him, especially women; he worked at the Alameda Naval Air Station doing stuff that required heavy lifting; he gambled a lot and drank too much; he dressed real nice, especially for his size; he was kind-hearted and foolish with money; if you caught him right after payday he would buy you dinner, even a suit of clothes if you asked him; he lived with a woman named Juanita; everything was in her name, the apartment, the car, everything—otherwise they wouldn't have anything; he could sing like Jerry Butler; a woman would have to be a fool to marry him; when he wasn't at work, you could usually find him at Esther's Orbit Room down on Seventh Street.

Bingo!

Miss Donna didn't know Big Josh's last name, at least that's what she told me, but I knew she was lying. Mama was going to be hot if she found out Miss Donna had told me as much as she had. Holding on to Big Josh's last name was Miss Donna's way of maintaining her gossip's integrity.

Big Josh was my last hope for getting the thirty-one dollars and fifty-two cents I needed to help Jessie Mae get home to her grandmother. I would find him, I told myself, explain Jessie Mae's dire circumstances, and he would reach his big hand into his big pocket and pull out big money—maybe one hundred dollars—just like that. Then he would tell me how pretty I was, how smart I was, and most of all how brave I was. He would tear up and say he would regret 'til his dying day that he wasn't the one raising me, and he envied Daddy because he was. I would crimp my lips in a thoughtful way, thank him, and turn around and walk away in carefully measured steps. I would not turn to wave even when it became evident that the sobbing I heard behind me was coming from him.

Of course, if Mama found out I'd had anything to do with Big Josh, she'd kill me. If Daddy found out I took money from Big Josh, it would kill Daddy. But I had no other choice. I had to try.

I waited until Mama was at Miss Donna's and Daddy was still at work before calling information and getting the number and address for Esther's Orbit Room.

"Hello, may I speak to Big Josh, please?"

"I'm sorry, baby; Big Josh works the swing shift now. We don't usually see him 'til 'round midnight. Can I take your number and have him call you?"

"Highgate four—uh, no, that is quite alright. Thank you so very much."

I hung up the phone and sat on the edge of my bed trying to regulate my breathing. That short call had drained me. It had taken me two whole days to get up the nerve just to look up the phone number for Esther's Orbit Room, and another two days to prepare for the call. At least I had covered my tracks. There was no way anybody would ever know I made that call. I didn't know if the woman who answered the phone was Esther or not, but I felt certain when she told Big Josh of the call, she would say, "Some white woman called for you."

Now I had no other choice. I had to go out and track down Big Josh.

It was really hard for me to break a rule, any rule. I was no Chantelle; I didn't think rules only applied to other people. I didn't resent rules. I liked them, actually. Following the rules was like playing "Mother, May I." I was good at it, and I usually won. But I was planning to break just about every one of Mama and Daddy's most important rules and a couple of the Ten Commandments, too. I was going to lie. I was going to sneak out of the house—at night. I was going to put myself in danger. And there was the possibility that I might even bring shame down on my whole family when somebody found my body, with no panties on, wrapped up in a burlap sack, and dumped in some alley.

I tried to think of other ways to save Jessie Mae, but I couldn't up with anything. I even tried reading the Bible for guidance, but Chantelle had read the pages with the nasty stuff so much, it kept falling open to them by itself. I asked myself what a hero would do. Mama was my biggest hero, though in many ways she was a lot like Chantelle; she did what she wanted. Mama would have to not do something to make her the kind of hero I needed. The women in the Civil Rights Movement I saw on TV doing sit-ins and marches, getting dogs sicced on them, and being blasted by fire hoses were heroes, but I didn't know their names. A hero without a name didn't count as much as a hero with one. I had read about Harriet Tubman and Sojourner Truth. They didn't bow down to slavery, but it seemed like it was easier to be a hero in those days when things were so messed up that heroes knew exactly what to do, like freeing the slaves. I bet even heroes were scared, at least the first time—well, maybe not Harriet Tubman.

Boy, was I scared. I was scared of getting caught. I was scared of getting a whuppin after I got caught. I was scared of not getting caught and having to go through with it. I was scared of all the unimaginable horrors that lurked outside at night. I was scared that I might not find Big Josh, and scared that I would. I was just plain scared. But I thought about Jessie Mae and how scared she must be. I thought about the Sheik and all the nasty things he was doing to her. And I thought about all the grown folks who, except for Daddy, didn't care enough to do anything, and I made up my mind.

CHAPTER 12

Sneaking out of the house at night wasn't a problem, once I made up my mind and talked myself into it. Chantelle had been sneaking out ever since boys started talking trash to her and she started listening. I had never tried it, but I knew it was easy. All you had to do was wait for Mama and Daddy to go bed, and listen for the sound of Marvin Gaye or Ray Charles to come drifting from their room. They were in for good after that. Sometimes, Daddy would come out to use the bathroom, but he always went right back to Mama, Marvin, and Ray. He wasn't scared anymore that I would spit up my formula and choke to death, so he didn't check on me like he used to when I was little.

I didn't have to worry about Chantelle telling on me, or suddenly remembering she was my big sister and trying to stop me, because the stuff the doctor gave her for her sprained ankle made her sleep like a zombie.

I stuffed some clothes under my bedcovers and patted them into a body shape. I tied my headscarf around a ball of rags and placed it on my pillow just so. I left the door open a crack so you could peek in without opening the door and see "me" in bed sound asleep.

Getting back in after sneaking out wasn't a problem either. Chantelle had a key that she hid in her penny jar. The problem was, what would I do once I got out there? How would I avoid all the late night dangers, such as the packs of wild dogs that roamed the streets of West Oakland? The one led by Red Eye Devil Dog was said to be especially vicious. He would chase you down, tear your ears from your head, rip the meat right off your bones, and swallow you in big chunks without even chewing.

How would I avoid the nasty men who liked to catch girls and do things to them, hurt them, even kill them like one of them did to poor, sweet Marianne Thomas when she was only seven years old?

Then there was Dracula, Frankenstein, and the Mummy. I wasn't much worried about Frankenstein; he was so big and clumsy you could see him coming a mile off. You had to be smart with him, though, and not run around like a fool and get cornered, because that's the only way he could catch you. The Mummy was even less of a worry than Frankenstein. He was kind of stupid—besides I'd never been to Egypt and dug up any pharaoh's tombs, so I figured I didn't have to worry about mummy curses.

But Dracula, that was a whole 'nother story. Dracula was the scariest white man in the history of the world. I wore a silver chain around my neck with a cross on it just because of him. I also had a crucifix—I got from Juanita Cuevas—that glowed in the dark. I used to hang it over my bed, but Chantelle complained its high-beam kept her awake, and I started keeping it under my pillow.

Different monster rules applied to Dracula. He could change into a bat, a wolf, or even another person. He could move faster than the eye could see. One minute you're alone, minding your own business, checking if you have titties or something, and the next minute he's behind you with his mouth wide open, spit dribbling out, ready to bite your neck, suck your blood, and turn you into something so ugly your own mama wouldn't recognize you.

You couldn't run from Dracula either. And if you wanted to make him stop messing with you, biting your mama, and your little kids, you had to kill him. You had to go right up into his house. You had to find his casket, and open it up. You had to look him in the face, and then you had to do something so horrible, I always squeezed my eyes shut when they did it in movies. It didn't seem fair you had to turn into a monster yourself in order to make the monster leave you alone.

Then there was the police. They were just about as bad as Dracula except wooden stakes didn't work on them.

The first night I sneaked out, I went three and one-half blocks, that's all—one half block down to West Grand, and three blocks over to Market. It was colder than I expected and spookier, too, with f fog drifting low on the ground transforming parked cars into humpbacked ghouls.

Big trucks rumbled by on West Grand going to the factories and warehouses that surrounded Chestnut Court. A few cars drove by. I tried to keep in the shadows close to buildings but doorways scared me. Parked cars scared me. Cars that slowed as the drivers peered through the fog scared me. I was ready to turn around, run home, confess everything to Daddy and Mama, and then take a nice hot bath and go to bed. But I wasn't crazy. There wouldn't be a nice hot bath for me, that's for sure. I urged myself on, promising if I just made it as far as Market Street I could go home. I didn't need to find Big Josh that night, I told myself. This was a scouting expedition like in the war movies.

I was a soggy mess by the time I crept all the way to Market. I tagged base on the light pole and turned around to scramble home. There was a swoosh sound at the back of my neck, and a rush of air like beating wings. There was a whine, and a metallic groan, and a figure shot out of the fog from behind me. I'm not ashamed to admit that I screamed. The figure made a sharp turn at full speed, spun around to face me, and screeched to a stop.

I felt my whole body liquefy.

The figure spoke. "What you doing out here by yourself?"

"None'a your business," I said like you're supposed to reply to boys when they get in your business. But I sure was glad to see Ol' Bad Richard. He hadn't been at school since that day Deirdre told on him and got him in trouble.

85

"Ain't you worried Raw Head 'n Bloody Bones gonna get ya?" Richard asked. Leaning on his bike, he was as relaxed with the night as I was stiff with fright.

I laughed a little too shrilly and said, "No." I put extra stress on the "no" drawing it out and adding a flick of chin to let him know how fearless I was. "Aren't you?"

"Shit," he said, drawing out the word until it was little more than a hiss.

"Come on," Richard said, "Um'a walk you home."

At least he didn't say he was *taking* me home. "You don't have to," I said, this time in a baby voice of relief.

"I know," he said.

"Why haven't you been at school?" I asked.

"I ain't got no time for no jive-ass honkies."

"What about your education?"

He laughed like I'd said something childish and cute.

"People dying so we can go to school and get an education," I continued, unable to stop myself.

"Um sorry for 'em. They dying for nothing, 'cause I ain't going."

His blasphemy almost struck me dumb.

"Tell me something, Miss Lady," he said. "What you gonna do with all that education once you get it?"

"I'm going to college, and then I'm getting a good job, and I'm going to buy me a house up in the hills . . ."

"Know what? You gon' still be a nigger."

That took my breath away. It was like being punched in the stomach. You called people niggers when you got in fights with them—*Um'a kick yo ass, nigger*—when you didn't respect them, believe them, or trust them—*Nigger, please!*—when you didn't like them, their mamas, their grandmama, or yourself—*Niggers ain't shit*—when you were too ignorant to know any better—You my nigger!—or you called them niggers when they were getting besides themselves, forgetting that they were down there in the bottom of the barrel with everybody else, and needed taking down a notch or two—*You gon' still be a nigger.*

Ol' Bad Richard didn't know me well enough to be talking to me like that. Mama and Daddy didn't use that word. And they didn't let us go around calling people niggers either. Daddy said when Negroes got lynched, the last thing they heard as their life was draining out was the word nigger.

We were *Negroes* and proud of it. Before that, Mama and Daddy had been *colored*, but not me and Chantelle. It took Chantelle a while to realize that she was even a Negro. For the longest time, until she was eight or nine, she thought people were saying *eagle*.

We didn't *show our color* when we went out. We spoke proper and kept our voices down. Our clothes were clean. Our legs weren't ashy, and our hair wasn't nappy. Our parents took care of us, and taught us the Lord's Prayer, and things like that. When our mama took us to Swan's or Housewives' Market, we didn't run all around, grabbing stuff off the shelves, causing the white man to raise his voice at us, and causing our mama to have to get up in his face.

Ol' Bad Richard didn't have anybody to teach him not to go around calling people niggers. His daddy was in jail, his mama was walking the streets, and his grandmother, Miss Bertha, was probably somewhere drunk.

A car drove past. It slowed, then backed up. An old man, about forty or fifty, leaned over the passenger side so he could talk through the open window. "Hey, li'l mama—"

Richard tore his face into something crazy and mean.

"Move on, mothafucka! This my ho."

He turned slightly to show the man his right hand jammed into his jacket pocket.

"No fault, no harm, young blood," the man said and drove off.

"I'm not a nigger, and I'm not a ho," I said, speaking so low I didn't think Richard would hear me. I wasn't talking to him anyway. I was talking to the whole wide world, especially old men who tried to hit on eleven-year-old girls.

Ol' Bad Richard said, "I had to say that to keep him off you. I know you ain't a—"

I stopped him, "That's okay."

He shot a glance over his shoulder. "We better get a move on."

He offered to let me ride his handlebars while he pumped, but I said no, that was okay. He told me I could have the seat, and he would stand up and pump. But I couldn't—I was just too soggy—so I said I would walk fast. He straddled his bike and coasted while I trotted beside him.

"Tell me the truth," he said. Why you out here? You call yourself running away?"

"Of course not. You know Josh—Big Josh?"

"Everybody know Big Josh."

"Well, he's my daddy. I'm looking for him."

"You lying. He not your daddy. Alex your daddy."

"Big Josh is my . . . *real* daddy." I hated saying that. Daddy was my real daddy, my only daddy. I waited for the cock to crow three times.

"Look girl, if that's all it is, why don't you just ask your mama?"

"Don't have to cop an attitude. I'm not supposed to know about Big Josh. It's some kinda family secret."

"So why you looking for him?"

"It's something real important. Life and death."

Richard snorted. "You wanna ask him what he getting you for Christmas?"

I said, "Pa-leeze!"

"You know you were going the wrong way, don't you?"

I didn't say anything. I didn't want him to know I was just practicing, trying to get used to being out in the dark. I didn't want him to know how scared I was. Besides, we were almost home and, although I had Chantelle's key, I was thinking about getting back in without getting caught.

"Want me to tell Big Josh you looking for him?"

"No, I gotta talk to him myself, and I don't want anybody to know about it."

"I'll take you, if you want me to, but not tonight."

"Okay." I was relieved I wouldn't have to brave the night alone again.

"Tomorrow night?" he asked.

I agreed.

Back at Chestnut Court, we walked around to the courtyard because it was easier to sneak in from the back than from the front.

"One more thing," Ol' Bad Richard said, "you can't go out at night looking like Shirley Temple. Try to look like a boy. Put some pants on and don't have your hair all hanging down your back like that."

He turned to leave, then stopped. I tossed my hair like Shirley Temple would have and waited.

"Tell Chantelle I said, hey," he said.

Chantelle. Always Chantelle.

"Chantelle doesn't need more *hay*," I said. "She has enough to last a lifetime.

CHAPTER 13

I started looking for Ol' Bad Richard as soon as it got good and dark. He hadn't told me what time he was coming so I went to the bedroom window every hour on the hour, and a few times in between, but I didn't see him down on the street waiting for me. I got ready for bed as usual, putting on my gown, and tying a scarf around my head. If he actually came, I planned to slip on a pair of dungarees, tuck my gown down into them, and cover it with the plaid shirt Mama wore when she helped Daddy clean the car. I would cover my headscarf with one of Daddy's knit caps.

When Ol' Bad Richard still hadn't come by ten o'clock, I started to worry. I needed to check the back to see if he was waiting for me there, but I had to get past Daddy first.

Mama was in bed, but it seemed like Daddy was going to stay up half the night on the couch reading *Native Son* for the six-hundredth and ninety-second time. I kept sneaking to the bedroom door and peeking out. Each time I checked, Daddy was there stretched out on the couch, the book propped up on his chest. Every once in a while he would lick a finger and turn a page or take a sip of his beer. "What's on your mind, Punkin?" Daddy asked without taking his eyes from the page.

"How you do that?"

"Do what?"

"See me when you weren't even looking in my direction?"

"You ain't slick."

I went into the room and sank down on the arm of the couch. "I can't sleep."

"Girl, get your behind off that arm."

I leaped up.

"Go get your blanket and come on out here with Daddy."

I got my blanket and scooted into the space Daddy made for me at the end of the couch. I wiggled in, pulled my knees up to my chin, and wrapped my blanket around me. I was as cozy as a papoose.

"Daddy, you ready?"

He said he was.

"Okay, how about . . . *cacophony?*"

"That's what you hear in the kitchen when your mama's pressing somebody's hair, and three or four sisters waiting their turn are just a-flapping their gums."

I had the hardest time smothering my laughter so I wouldn't wake up the whole building. When I had myself halfway under control, I said, "That was funny, Daddy. Now give me the real definition."

"Oh, you want the white man's definition, too. You should have said so, Punkin." Daddy closed his eyes and recited, "Cacophony: a discordant and meaningless mixture of sounds."

I batted my eyes and said, "Why sir, I do believe you've again been imbibing of *Webster's* sweet nectar."

"That I have, my li'l chickadee, that I have," Daddy replied. "Your turn. Here goes . . . *gambol.*"

"To bet on something. Uh . . . to play a game of chance."

"You jumped on that one, but you didn't let me finish. Remember what I told you about homonyms?"

"Okay, okay. Gambol . . . gambol: to skip around playfully, tra-la-la-la."

Daddy reached over and gave me five. He smelled like Royal Crown pomade and Palmolive soap. The beer on his breath smelled like buttermilk. I felt like his Punkin. Daddy started talking about Richard Wright, Bigger Thomas, and giant rats. I nodded and said,

91

"Umm," a couple of times; then I fell asleep.

I dreamed of doing battle with giant rats armed with extension cords. Jessie Mae was in the dream. She just stood there looking all hangdog while I wore myself out trying to protect the two of us from the horde of rats. "It's no use," she said. "It's too late. You done messed up."

The next day and the day after that I looked all over for Ol' Bad Richard. I couldn't find him anywhere. I asked everybody at school if they'd seen him and nobody had. I finally had to stop asking when Deirdre starting spreading lies about me—saying I "liked" him and I was looking for him so we could "do it." I kept on looking though. I heard talk that he was in juvie. When I asked his friend, Darnell, about it, he just shrugged.

I was desperate to find Ol' Bad Richard, desperate to help Jessie Mae get away, and desperate to stop the dreams. I had to find Big Josh, and I had to do it fast before a monster in one of my dreams caught me, or something even worse happened to Jessie Mae.

No Ol' Bad Richard meant no protection. The next best thing was a bike. A bike could go fast. It could take short cuts cars couldn't. It could help me get away from all kinds of monsters, including old men. I needed a bike, and I knew where to go to get one—at Miss Bea's place. Her apartment was across the courtyard on the second floor opposite ours. After school I went to do business with Artie and James, brothers, business partners, and two of Miss Bea's seven kids. Instead of cutting across the courtyard, I went the long way so Mama wouldn't see me.

Cupping my hands around my mouth, I made a whoop, whoop, whoop sound under their window. It was stupid, but that was their secret code. I had to use it or they would have ignored me. Well, maybe it wasn't so secret—every kid in Chestnut Court knew it and probably a few grown folks did too.

Artie came out onto the landing and leaned over the railing. He said, "Hey." I said "Hey" back. He said, "What's happening?" I said, "Nothing much." Then we didn't say anything for a while.

Artie was twelve years old and fat. He had a deep voice for a kid, and it sounded deeper than usual and scratchy.

Fat kids in our neighborhood were usually nervous kids. The favorite pastime of bad kids was beating them up. If you were fat, you had to fight your way home from school just about every day. Sometimes six or seven kids followed the fat kid home, slinging insults and taunts or running past to punch him.

But Artie was one fat kid who wasn't nervous in the least. That was because he and James invented their own fighting system. They called it the "High John the Conqueror Whup-Ass System" in honor of their mother, Miss Bea, who was into working roots and who could whup some butts too. The secret of their system: Lone Ranger and Daffy Duck. Those were the characters on a couple of old, beat up, little kids' lunch pails that Artie and James carried with them everywhere they went.

Artie was the brain who thought up the system and put it together. All it took was a small bag of quick-set cement he bought with his own money and mixed in one of Miss Bea's good mixing bowls. After he filled the pails with cement, sealed the lids shut and let the cement get hard, he and James could take out two or three bad kids at a time with one swing of their "lunch chucks." They only had to use them once or twice before the bad kids got the message. After that, nobody messed with them. They had enough power to be bad kids if they had wanted to, but they were too kind—all of Miss Bea's children were—and besides, Artie was more interested in making money than in being bad.

James came out and squeezed in at the railing next to his brother.

You never saw one without the other; now, the set was complete.

"Can I borrow your bike for a couple of hours tonight?" I asked Artie.

"Naw," he said. "I need it to deliver my papers."

"Come on. I won't keep it long."

"You gon' deliver my papers?"

I laughed.

"Um serious."

James weighed in. "Ma'dear said he can't do his route 'cause he sick. Five hundred and ninety-nine—that's his temperature."

Artie nudged him affectionately. "Aw, be quiet boy. You know how big a thermometer have to be to measure that high?"

James nudged him back. One of them farted. They giggled. One tried to fan the odor toward the other.

"I'll pay you," I said.

But they were so caught up in their fart follies they didn't hear me.

I raised my voice. "Two dollars. I'll pay you two dollars you let me borrow your bike tonight for a couple of hours."

"Five," Artie said. A fit of coughing grabbed him, shook him, bent him over, and had him gasping for breath. He coughed until his eyes watered. It sounded like his lungs were clogged with Jell-O. James pounded on his back, though that didn't seem to help. Artie's coughing finally let up a bit; then it wheezed to a stop. He stepped over to the garbage chute and spat into it a mouthful of something that was as thick and gooey as Jell-O.

"Five dollars and it's yours tonight and tomorrow."

"I just need it a couple of hours. Three dollars."

Artie eyed me, trying to assess how much he could get out of me.

I said, "That's all I have."

He took the deal.

"But she a girl!" James protested.

"She knows that, man," Artie said. "She need any help, you gon' help her, ain't you?"

James said, "Oh, man."

Artie stared at him until he relented and said, "Okay."

Artie asked me where I was going, and I told him.

"You'll be alright if you fix up like a boy. When you get here tonight, me and James'll have some stuff together for you to wear.

I unbraided my hair, combed it out, and stood in front of the bathroom mirror a long time looking at myself, trying to memorize what I looked like with a head full of hair. Then I parted it down the middle and braided it into two braids. When Mama did my hair, she braided underhand, and the braids hung down my back like they were supposed to. I didn't know how to do underhand, so my braids stuck out like my girl, Pipi Longstockings.

I stared at my reflection, passing the scissors from hand to hand, trying to make myself do it, trying to make myself cut off my hair. I was having a hard time giving up the only part of me that was worth anything; that set me apart; that made me special; that prompted old ladies to ask, "Child, where'd you get such a pretty head of hair?"; that caused girls at school to fuss over me, braiding and rebraiding my hair, or letting me cut in line in front of them so they could play with it.

Without my hair I was nobody, just another Negro child wandering around in the dark.

Step on a crack, break your mother's back.

I had stepped on so many cracks, crossed so many lines—sneaking out of the house at night, lying, messing around in Mama's business—I'd done enough to fracture just about every bone in Mama's body. Now I was stepping on another crack, crossing one more line. Pretty soon I'd cross over the line that made me her child. She would disown me, beat me half to death, and then send me down

South to live with some of her people where I would have to eat hog maws and use outhouses.

It wasn't fair. None of it was. I was good. I did what they told me, even when Chantelle and other kids made fun of me. And I was always scared of messing up, always scared of making Mama mad, terrified of getting the mess beat out of me. When it came down to it, I would rather make Dracula mad than Mama.

It wasn't fair that grown folks owned us, made us do what they wanted even if it wasn't what we wanted, even if what they wanted was bad. It wasn't fair that grown folks thought they could do anything to a kid and get away with it, and it wasn't fair that other grown folks let them.

"Bump this!" I said out loud. Then I lifted the scissors to my head and cut off the first braid. There was no physical pain. I felt wicked. And I liked it. I wrapped a rubber band around the end of the severed braid so it wouldn't come loose when I used it later.

Then I cut off the other one.

CHAPTER 14

That night at 11:30, Artie and James were waiting for me on the street side of their building next to the clump of bushes shaped like Donald Duck, just as they had promised. They wore jackets over their pajamas and knit caps pulled down to their eyes. James had his sockless feet stuck in a pair of Gallenkamp brogans while Artie sported fuzzy baby blue house shoes.

"I know," he said when he saw me trying not to stare at them. "Ma'dear makes me wear them 'cause'a my cold."

Artie handed me a Swan's shopping bag. "Here, put these on."

I took the bag and pulled out an old pair of navy blue corduroy pants that had a hole in the knee.

"Just put them on over your pedal pushers," he said. *Capris!* I wanted to scream to correct him. But I took the pants and climbed into them. The waist fit me like a hula hoop.

Artie said, "Give her the belt, man." James handed me an old piece of rope. I threaded it through the belt loops and tied it in front in a bow. James said, "Aw, man."

"You gotta tie it in a double knot," Artie said, using the same tone he used with James when he was explaining something very basic to him.

"Now, put this on over your car coat," he said, handing me an old army jacket. He leaned back and surveyed the effect. "Hat," he called out.

James took off his knit cap and handed it to him.

I shook my head.

"You can't go out in that head rag."

"Scarf," I said.

"Okay," Artie said, "scarf. Still makes you look like a girl."

"Yeah! Like Aunt Jemima," seconded James just before he snatched my scarf and darted out of reach.

I clutched my head in my hands. "Give me that back!"

Artie peered at me in the dark. "What did you do?

"I cut my hair . . ."

"You jacked yourself," James said.

Don't laugh, man," Artie said, "she has feelings, too."

"I'll get the clippers," James suggested.

"Yeah, but be careful you don't wake nobody up."

James returned with a pair of hand clippers, the kind that worked when you squeezed the handles together.

I backed up until I could feel the Donald Duck bush grabbing at me; but in the end, I let him cut my hair down to even it out. Artie stood back with his hand on his chin and examined his work. James copied him.

"What you think?" Artie asked.

Good thing she don't have no titties," James said.

Artie elbowed James in his ribs. "That ain't nice. Say you're sorry."

"I'm sorry you don't—"

Artie jabbed him again.

They agreed I could pass for a boy as long as I stayed on the bike and didn't talk.

"Here's the repair kit, and there's a pump on the other side," Artie said, pointing to the bike bag slung over the rear fender. "You know how to fix flats, don't ya?"

I nodded a silent lie.

"Okay. There's a spare chain on the other side and a flashlight."

"What I need a spare chain for?"

"Sometimes," James explained, "they break when you jump a

curb—"

"Or when you try to ride down the stairs," Artie added.

James dropped his head and said, "Oh, man."

"Take Adeline to Seventh Street," Artie advised. "When you get to Seventh, turn right and go all the way down. You can't miss it; you'll see the lights and people and stuff. You sure you don't want James to go with you?"

I said I didn't.

Artie said, "Well, go fast. Don't act scared. Act like you know where you going and you wish somebody would mess with you."

"Yeah, act like you going to the store to get some snuff for your grandmama," James said.

Artie punched him. James farted.

I took off.

I pumped hard and fast. I stood on the pedals and glided silently through the night air. I acted like I knew where I was going, and I wasn't scared, and after a while I actually wasn't. The wind whistling past my face felt so good I wanted to whoop as loud as I could, shout something silly at the sky, make motorcycle noises.

The first time I went out at night I was too scared to see much of anything. This time I saw things I hadn't noticed that first night. Parked cars no longer looked like monsters, even when big puffs of fog floating close to the ground bumped into them and absorbed them into their mist. I saw quiet houses all lit up with Christmas lights and a few wiry stray cats. A car would roll by now and then but the drivers didn't seem to notice me. None of them slowed down. I saw a man peeing at the side of a liquor store, a woman scrubbing her front steps, a car stopped in the middle of an intersection with three women working frantically under its hood.

When I came to DeFremery Park at Sixteenth Street, I was struck by how the night transformed it into a magical patch of damp green, lit with the dandelion glow of streetlights. Four boys sat at a picnic table—their bikes leaning against it—as they drank something from a brown paper bag, passing it among themselves. One of the boys saw me glide past.

"Hey, gimme that bike, punk!" he yelled.

I forced myself to count to ten before doing any getaway pumping. The boys hopped on their bikes like a posse and came after me. I cut over to the street so I wouldn't have to worry about slowing down at corners or jumping curbs. I shot through red lights like a bandit. Stop signs, yield signs, the-family-that-prays-together-stays-together signs were there to cheer me on, boost my speed. When I hit Tenth Street, the posse was more than a block and a half behind me. But Tenth Street was where I messed up. A car full of winos thought they had the right to run stop signs, too. If I hadn't looked back to see where the posse was, I would have seen the winos in time to turn in their direction and avoid a crash. Instead, I barely had a second to clamp down on the handbrakes and, the next thing I knew, I was on the ground.

The posse came up on me fast after that. I struggled to my feet and was trying to get back on the bike when one of them shoved me from behind. I went down again, and the bike came down on top of me. The repair kit, pump, and chain slid out of the bike bag. I grabbed for them. My fear of losing Artie's stuff was blown way out of proportion, considering everything else that I might have lost at that moment.

One of the boys said, "Take the fuckin bike and let's book."

I grabbed on to Artie's bike and screamed, "No!"

"Say, leave her alone. She's a girl," another of the boys said.

I recognized the voice. It was Darnell from my class, Ol Bad Richard's buddy.

Another boy who was short and stocky and sporting something

between a bad conk and a moisture-damaged press-and-curl said, "Um gone make her suck my cock."

Darnell wouldn't look at me, but he said, "Come on, Alwin man, leave her alone."

"What you gone do? You a punk? You wanna suck it."

The other two boys laughed. Darnell said, "Naw, fuck, naw."

Alwin grabbed his thing through his pants and shook it at me. The boys laughed, including Darnell.

One hundred years from now, if you ask me what went through my mind, why I did what I did, I still won't be able to explain it. The most truthful answer I can offer is . . . I don't know. What I can tell you is never in my whole, entire life had I been so scared. Also, never in my whole, entire life had I been so angry. And it wasn't just Alwin shaking his funky li'l thing in my face—talking about making me suck it—it was a whole lot of things, so many things I couldn't begin to name them. In fact, until that moment, I hadn't even known I was angry. I guess I had taken all the angry stuff and pushed it inside me, way down deep in the basement, too close to the furnace and, thanks to Alwin, it caught fire and exploded.

I saw the blood spray from Alwin's mouth, and the other boys scrambling to get out of the way, but it took me a while to connect the effect with a cause and to realize I was that cause—I and the bike chain I was swinging like a Titan, left and right, cutting him to chunks to be swallowed whole. Even when he was on the ground, trying to crawl away, I kept swinging. When the boys screamed at me, pleaded, "Stop! You're killing him," I kept swinging and slicing and swinging and slicing until Alwin managed to crawl out of my reach.

His friends got him up and helped him straddle his bike. Then, with one on each side of him to keep him upright, they wobbled away. One of the boys looked back over his shoulder and said, "I don't care if you is a girl. You done messed with the wrong muthafucka."

Darnell didn't leave with them. "I'm sorry," he said, still avoiding my eyes. "He wasn't really going to make you do nothing. He just talks a lot of trash."

I refused to acknowledge him. Sorry wasn't enough anymore. I busied myself checking Artie's bike, making sure there were no damages I would have to pay for and stuffing the repair kit and chain back into the bike bag.

"Link and Bam Jackson's Alwin's brothers," Darnell said.

I gave him a look that said, "So."

"They practically grown men. When Alwin gets home and they see what he look like, they gon' come back and make him fight you. If they tired or in a hurry, they gon' beat you up they selves just to get it over with."

I ignored him. We were classmates, which was just about as close to being friends as a boy and girl in elementary school could get, and he had laughed at me when he should have been on my side. I had absolutely no need for him now.

"You gotta hide," he pleaded. "They gon' be back."

I wasn't listening. I stood there smiling like I didn't have a sense in my head. It had just dawned on me—I didn't need to pee.

But I wasn't stupid, and I wasn't a fool, either. I knew who Link and Bam Jackson were. I'd heard the stories about them and their thirteen brothers and sisters. I knew I was in trouble. Big trouble. And I didn't need Mr. Darnell Chicken Shit Davis to tell me that.

Darnell jerked around looking up and down the street as though he expected Link and Bam Jackson to materialize suddenly out of no-where like Dracula.

"Come on," insisted Mr. Chicken Shit, "we can hide in my old house. It's all boarded up, but I know a secret way in."

We were at Tenth Street. Darnell and his bike were pointed toward Union Street where he used to live before the city moved the

Negroes out of that part of West Oakland for what they called urban redevelopment, and what Daddy called "Negro Eradication." Since redevelopment started and they moved everybody out, his old house and mine, too, had been sitting vacant for years. I didn't want to set foot in some old, falling-down house that was full of rats, and the very same roaches that were there before people moved out. Besides winos and hobos lived in some of those houses, now.

"You coming or not?" Darnell demanded.

I said I wasn't, and he took off without another word. Good riddance. I had a better idea. Before I would take a chance hiding in an old house that might be full of winos and hoboes, I would go to one of the old houses that I knew had winos sleeping in it. But at least they were family—Cut'n Ollie and his son Reno—Mama's cousins, the only father/son team of winos I had ever heard of and the current residents of our old house.

CHAPTER 15

I switched on the flashlight, and pushing Artie's bike I squeezed my way along the side of our old house trying to avoid the broken glass, jagged pieces of concrete, and dog doo-doo. When I made it to the backyard I was greeted by a pitiful sight. Our poor old house leaned one way and the back porch leaned another. The house looked like somebody had poked out its eyes. A tree seemed to be growing out of its roof. When the wind blew, winter dried stalks of weeds standing nearly as tall as me made a spooky sound, moving and shaking, like they were whispering to one another, snickering about something mean and nasty.

I leaned Artie's bike against what was left of the falling down back porch with collapsed stairs. It made me sad to see my old house looking so beat-up and uncared for. I wanted to sit down and spend some time with it. Tell it how sorry I was for leaving it all by itself with nobody to love it. But I was in a hurry, and, besides, I could hear wino-snoring all the way outside. So I climbed through a ground-floor window into the room that used to be Mama and Daddy's when I was little and life wasn't so complicated.

Cut'n Ollie was laid out on a dirty old quilt with his pants pulled down to his knees and his big ol' yellow butt glowing in the beam of my flashlight. He had on one shoe and one sock—on opposite feet. His pockets were pulled inside out. I shook his shoulder. "Cut'n Ollie. Cut'n Ollie, please wake up. I need your help."

He made a snorting noise, but he didn't wake up. I wondered if Reno had taken all his money and left him like that. Poor Cut'n Ollie. He was the sweetest person I knew when he wasn't drunk. I tugged enough of the blanket from underneath him to cover his butt. Then I sat on the windowsill to think.

I was all scraped up, there was a hole in both knees of Artie's pants now, and one of my knees was bleeding. That was one big whooptee compared to the other stuff I had to worry about. I didn't know how long I would have to hide or how I would know when it was safe to come out. I tried to ignore the things I heard scurrying about in the corners of the room and the strange noises the house was making that sounded like the noises houses made in monster movies. I fingered the crucifix hanging around my neck, though Dracula was far from my thoughts. I was not as concerned about movie monsters as I was about real-life people, such as whoever robbed Cut'n Ollie. What if he came back for the other shoe? And then there was Link and Bam.

It was better, I decided, to face monsters out in the open where you had room to run rather than in spooky old houses, even if the spooky old house used to be yours. But before I could leave I had to check one thing. I took a deep breath and sucked up my courage and let it flow through my muscles and tendons and bones all the way up to the top of my head and all the way down to my baby toes. Then I set out to walk the ten feet from Mama and Daddy's old room to the one Chantelle and I used to share when we were little.

Ten feet may not seem like it is very far when you're strolling through a field full of daisies under a bright sun with birds singing and butterflies fluttering by. But try walking ten feet in a ghost house where stuff from the ceiling drops down on your neck and it's hard to brush it off, where each step makes the floor creak and every creak is echoed over and over until you can't tell if it's the one you made in the first place or one somebody else is making. Ten feet can take eleven years to walk. But I had to see our old room. I had to prove to myself that it had actually existed, that it wasn't one of those "once upon a time" things. I had to prove to myself that there was a time and a place where I had been happy and felt safe, even if the happiest, safest, place was now smack dab in the middle of the scariest place, ever. There was a word for this, a word for things that switch on you, things that mean the same and opposite at the same time. Daddy would know that word, but I couldn't think of it. I didn't try. I needed all my senses to walk those ten feet.

At first I thought the flashlight was playing tricks on my eyes or maybe the room had actually shrunk—though I knew that wasn't possible, not in real life anyway. But the room I remembered was so much larger than the one I was peering into. The room I remembered had been huge, gigantic. The one I was looking at was little more than a closet. I didn't see how me and Chantelle had fit in there, even in the days when we both were shaped like Easter eggs and titties hadn't yet come between us.

I edged into the room far enough to shine the flashlight behind the door. It was still there, my safe. A hole in the wall that I had enlarged, smoothing out its edges with the handle of a brush. All my *me stuff* was stored in that hole—the good stuff, the bad stuff, the stuff I wanted to keep and remember forever. I secretly deposited my first baby tooth there, before I found out how valuable they were, before I knew anything about a "tooth fairy" who paid fifty-five cents a tooth. The first book I learned to read, *The Poky Little Puppy*, was in there too, rolled tightly into a tube so none of the "sweet joy of knowing the sacred art of reading" could escape. There was a Popsicle stick in there. The stick had a piece of paper wrapped around it. On the paper was a picture of little Marianne Thomas lying in her tiny little casket. The paper was wrapped tightly around the stick and held in place by a rubber band so none of the Marianne's terror or her family's grief could escape. I wanted to put something in the hole for Jessie Mae. But I was wearing somebody else's clothes, and I didn't have a thing to offer. I turned to leave and stopped. Gripping the flashlight between my knees, I reached up behind my neck and unclasped the silver chain and dropped it and the cross into the hole.

I went back to where Cut'n Ollie was. I poked him with my toe, trying one more time to wake him up. It was no use. I was on my own. I climbed back out the window and got Artie's bike.

I stopped at the corner of the house to patch together enough courage to go back to the streets. Just as I had talked myself into going out into the open, a slow moving car, with its lights off, turned the corner from Tenth Street. I sprouted about sixteen thumbs, fumbling with the flashlight trying switch it off. It leaped from my hands like something wild and hid itself in the weeds. I dropped to a squat searching for it just as a blast of light hit the house. I ducked lower, burying my head in the weeds. The car pulled to a stop, its lights pinning me among the rubble and dog doo-doo.

Had they spotted me? Blood rushed to my head. The roaring in my ears drowned out all sound. I couldn't tell what was happening, but I didn't dare lift my head to find out. I thought I heard a car door open and close, and it was all I could do to keep from bolting from my hiding place, running wildly, and screaming for my mama. I had taken myself out of Mama's protection, though, when I left her house, and now I was on my own. After about ten thousand years, the light began to move slowly until the car got to the next house and stopped.

I stayed where I was—head down, butt up—until the car moved to the third house; then I got moving. The flashlight had gone out, but I patted around in the weeds until I found it. I headed back to the rear of the house dragging the bike. When I got there I forced myself to stand still, close my eyes, and think. The longer I held still, the clearer my mind became. I could feel my body vibrating like an engine burning fear. My heart was thumping like the one in that Edgar Allan Poe story. All the Jacksons had to do was turn the radio down, open the windows, stick their heads out, and surely they would have heard it.

I was breathing through my mouth, and the night air tasted gray like the fog. And behind my eyelids I could see Filbert Street just as clear as day.

I could see the Jacksons cruising up one side of the street and down the other, checking out each boarded up house. If I went back to the street they would see me. Once they saw me, it was all over.

Catastrophe. Disaster. Doom.

What would Harriet Tubman do?

Harriet Tubman had a gun, stupid.

So.

Okay, okay—Think!

Harriet Tubman went underground.

I was a little more than a block away from Seventh Street. Esther's Orbit Room was all the way down at the other end of Seventh, nearly ten blocks away. I had to get to Esther's, but I had to stay off the streets. I couldn't fly, and I couldn't swing from vines like Tarzan. The fences separating the backyards leaned every which way. Some lay flat on the ground. They were perfect bridges between the yards. I would work my way through the middle of the block, backyard to backyard—my underground—crossing streets only when it was absolutely necessary. I pushed the bike under the falling-down porch and piled up some trash in front of it. Then I took off on foot.

I stopped in one yard and climbed on top of a brick incinerator that people who lived there before had used to burn garbage. I stood on my toes and stretched, straining to catch sight of the Jackson brothers. I could see the streets in both directions. I didn't see the Jacksons. Either they had given up and gone home or they were out there somewhere with their lights off waiting for me to show myself. There was one more possibility that was almost too scary to think about—maybe they weren't even in the car. Maybe they were out hunting on foot—coming at me from different directions.

Each time a car passed on Adeline Street I nearly swallowed my tongue. Then I saw the Jacksons' car as it turned off Filbert onto Eighth Street and was heading toward Adeline going just as slow as before. Its lights were off again. They would be a couple of blocks away by the time I passed through the block and had to cross Adeline.

It was tough going, scaling those fences that still stood, keeping out of patches of tangled weeds and vines, avoiding planks with old, rusty nails sticking out of them, ignoring spider webs and, all the while, expecting something to grab me at any minute. I stepped into a hole full of something wet and slimy and nearly screamed. When I pulled out my foot it smelled like I had been playing kickball with a rotten cabbage, and I squished when I walked.

I felt it before I heard it, a low rumble that blended with the noise from the Nimitz Freeway, vibrating in my breastbone. I finally heard it when it grew louder and changed into a wet growl that seemed to be coming from all directions at once. All I could think of was getting as far away as I could, climbing somewhere high—a rooftop, a telephone pole, anything that was out of its reach. Without realizing it I was running. Running and stumbling. Crawling at times. Stepping on stuff. Stepping in stuff. Forgetting about dog doo-doo, sinkholes full of slime, and rusty nails. I didn't care how much noise I made—I was trying to get away from the Devil Dog., If I didn't get away I wasn't going to die all quiet like.

I was nearly at the fence that meant freedom when I passed into the funk zone. The nastiest thing I had ever smelled hit me in the face, taking my breath away for a second. Someone must have dug a pit to use as a bathroom. I couldn't see it, but my nose told me it was near. Suddenly the growl stopped, and I knew my time was up. Without knowing exactly where the pit was, I leaped for the fence. I landed hard, face down on dry ground, on the wrong side—the growling side—of the bathroom pit. The growl clamped on to my left pant leg. I tried to jerk loose, but it was no use. I was caught. It was dragging me backward.

I grabbed fistfuls of dirt, dried up weeds, anything in my path, trying to keep out of the jaws of the Devil Dog. Somehow, I managed to flip over onto my back. When I saw it I nearly gave up. It was one of those big, raggedy looking dogs. It was mixed with so many different kinds of dogs, it looked like it had been patched together by Dr. Frankenstein. It looked like it had never been a puppy. It looked like you could confuse it with just a pat on the head and a kind word. It was one of those dogs that was just plain ol' mean. But a glimmer of hope reached me from somewhere. I kicked hard with my free foot and inched backward. Another kick, another inch. My hand touched something, a plank. I clutched at it, but it was firmly attached to something and I couldn't get it loose. I kicked again. My pants ripped. It was the most beautiful sound. I kicked again and I was free—for the moment. I scrambled to my feet and ran for the fence. My leap was more successful this time, and I cleared the stink hole, landing at the foot of the fence.

The Devil Dog lunged at me. But the clothesline knotted around his neck and tied to a dead tree, stopped him midair, and slammed him to the ground.

That was it for me. I went back to my old house and dragged Artie's bike from under the porch. I stood there in the dark for a few minutes, maybe an hour, maybe more waiting for my heart to settle back into its place in my chest and for my breathing to even out. Then I straightened my clothes, tightened my rope belt, and brushed as much dirt, twigs, and dried weeds from my clothes as I could. The last thing I did before going back to the street was to snatch the knit cap from my head and stuff it into my pocket.

CHAPTER 16

I hadn't gone far when a blast of light hit me from behind so suddenly I nearly fell. Squealing tires and the roar of a monster engine choked away my breath. For a second I considered covering my ears with my hands, squeezing my eyes shut, and falling to the ground whimpering. That thought quickly passed, and I jumped on the bike, lowered my head, and pedaled fast. But I couldn't outrun, or in this case, outpedal, a car, and I knew it.

The car sped up and shot past me. At the end of the street it swung around crossways, blocking my escape. A tall guy and one a little shorter got out of the front doors. A much shorter, stocky one with a bad conk got out of the back. They leaned against the car waiting for me.

I had learned my lesson about squeezing the handbrakes too hard, and I had no intention of launching myself over the handlebars again. In fact, I had no intention of stopping at all. Going fast felt too good. I felt powerful, more powerful than I had ever felt in my life. I could keep going and no one or nothing could stop me, not Link, not Bam, not their big ol' car just sitting there.

I was sick of people pushing me around, sick of trying to help Jessie Mae and getting nowhere, and sick of running and hiding. Maybe Jessie Mae was right, maybe it was too late. Maybe it was too late for her and for me, too. It definitely was too late for me to turn back. Too late for do overs.

I don't know when they realized I wasn't going to stop. I saw Link look at Bam and then both started scrambling to get back into the car. Alwin had already sneaked into the backseat. I smiled. I threw back my

111

head and howled. Then I stood up to pedal faster.

Two things kept me from crashing into that car: First, I was angry, I mean really angry. I was even angrier than when I was slicing Alwin with my chain—and I wanted to savor it, roll it around in my mouth and enjoy the bitterness of it. I wanted somebody to mess with me. I wanted to take that bike chain and the bitterness and destroy faces, slice through them with three quick snaps the way Mama folded towels. That bike chain and my anger were going to make up for every salty, sour thing I'd ever had stuffed down my gullet, ever had to swallow because I was a child, or a girl, or scared. Second, I was very aware that I wasn't on my own bike—I was getting ready to crash Artie's bike and that wouldn't be right. He had never done anything but be nice to me. But, I didn't slow down.

When I was close enough to make out the welts on Alwin's face, I stopped pedaling and rode the wind the rest of the way. I squeezed the handbrakes rhythmically in quick short bursts. I locked eyes with the Jackson brother behind the steering wheel, and I smiled. He cut his wheels to the right to avoid me, and I cut my wheel in the same direction, skidding into the turn. He was the bullfighter, I was the bull. I squeezed the brakes tighter, and this time my tires squealed. I slid tighter into the radius of his turn and held my place. His eyes tightened. Sweat poked out of his face like glass zits. He knew if he messed up on our little dance, if he mistimed it and our pass was too fast or just a little too slow, he stood a good chance of doing time at San Quentin.

When I slowed down enough for them to stop, the Jacksons climbed out of the car a little slower than they had earlier. The tall one grabbed Alwin by the scuff of his neck and slung him at me.

"Take care of your business, man, so we can go home."

I stood ready with my chain. Alwin made a couple of tentative steps toward me but refused to come within reach. The shorter brother, the one with the broad shoulders and knock knees, shoved Alwin out of the way and spat on the ground. "Um sick'a this shit," he said. Then he came at me fast. I sucked my lower lip between my teeth and trapped it there. I wrapped a length of chain around my fist and braced myself. Knock Knees was almost within reach when he skidded to a stop. "Hold up!" he said. Without talking his eyes off me, he beckoned for his brothers to join him. As a group, they bent over and peered at me. "This here's a girl! Alwin, man, you let a girl do this to you?"

As "suck my cock" wouldn't have gone over with his brothers, Alwin was having trouble thinking of what to say.

"Get your punk ass back in the car," one of the brothers said, and Alwin did as he was told.

The tall one approached me. "Hey, li'l sis," he said, "these streets ain't no place for you. Put your bike in the trunk. We'll take you where you're going."

He reached for the bike, and I swung at him, just missing but getting close enough for a clean shave.

"Okay. Okay. Tell you what, you get on your bike and go on where you going. We'll hang back a little and follow you in case some other fool tries to mess with you—and believe me, one will. When you get where you going or you get tired of us following you, just wave and we'll go about our business. Okay?"

I didn't agree or disagree. I got back on Artie's bike and pedaled as hard as I could. Every block or so, I shot a glance over my shoulder, and they were still there with their lights on low, going slow enough to stay behind me, running lights if they had to keep up. After a while I stopped checking.

I pedaled down Seventh Street toward where the sky was all lit up. The closer I got, the brighter the lights got until I was in the midst of a dancing parade of neon and flashing lights. It seemed that thousands of people crowded the sidewalks, crossing the street wherever they pleased. I marveled that so many people found so much to do so late at night. I saw more Cadillacs in more colors in one place than I'd ever seen before. I saw men who looked like movie stars—Negro men, men handsomer than Harry Belafonte and Sidney Poitier. And I saw women as pretty as Mama, but dressed way nicer with fox stoles and everything. I saw barbershops, beauty parlors, fancy restaurants, and bars, and it seemed there was a shoeshine stand on every block.

Merry Christmas, baby. You sho' did treat me right.

I was in a world spun of music. It drifted near the ground like fog, floated overhead like low-lying clouds, wafted from every doorway. From somewhere not too far away, I smelled barbecue. I felt if I turned my head in the right direction and cocked it just so, I could smell the music, too. And it would have been sweet, tangy, and saucy, like the barbecue.

As I looked around, I got angry again. How come nobody had told me about Seventh Street? All my life I thought it was a place where winos and hoochie-coochie women hung out, but in real life, it was more like New York on New Year's Eve like I'd seen on TV.

I put my cap back on and walked the crowded sidewalk pushing Artie's bike. I was a boy and nobody gave me a second look. When I came to Esther's Orbit Room, I leaned the bike against a streetlight. I had forgotten about Link and Bam until they cruised by, and the one driving tapped the horn. I waved. Then I pushed open the door to the part of the building that looked like a café and went straight to a waitress lady. Daddy always took off his hat to show respect when he went inside a building, but no way was I going to take off my cap.

Before I could speak, the waitress lady said, "What you doing out on the streets this time a'night, baby?" She had a lot of auntie kindness in her voice, along with a bit of "straighten up and answer me."

I got nervous for a minute, but then I remembered I was a boy—a bad boy—and I had the right to be anywhere I wanted, any time I wanted. I stuck out my stomach, made my voice deep, and asked for Big Josh. The hostess lady cocked her head to the side and looked at me for so long I started feeling damp and itchy and had to cross my legs.

When she said, "You still ain't answered my question," everything that was holding me up started to wobble.

"Looking for Big Josh," I repeated in my own voice. She sighed and led me to a table in the corner. "You stay here, baby" she said and left.

I checked out the room, hoping to find somebody who looked vaguely the way I imagined Big Josh would. The room was long with low ceilings and muted lights. The door to the street was slightly to the left of where I sat. A bell hung over it. Every once in a while I swiveled my head to the left to check the door, just in case the bell was broken, or you couldn't hear it over the jukebox that seemed to be playing Marvin Gaye's, "How Sweet It Is to Be Loved by You," over and over.

Three taxi cab drivers sat at a table across from me. They were eating fried pork chops, scrambled eggs, and waffles. Every three or four chews the darkest one would hold up his fork to get the others attention and recite a line from *The Signifying Monkey*. They'd laugh and then fall back to eating. Fork goes up: "The monkey said, 'Muthafucka, can't you see? Why, you standin' on my goddamn feet!'" Fork goes down. They eat. Fork goes up: "The lion said, 'I ain't heard a word you said. If you say three more I'll be steppin on yo muthafuckin head!'" I slapped my hands over my mouth. I had never heard *The Signifying Monkey* done like that. Uncle Fred didn't use curse words in his version, and it was funny, but the taxi cab driver's version was way better.

Some really good-looking ladies sat at another table laughing and talking and drinking coffee. They had on red nail polish and matching lipstick, and their hair was all done up. They looked like they were on their way to a party. I wished I was going with them instead of sitting there waiting, hoping for "happily ever after" to waft in the next time the door opened. I had fought my way to Esther's Orbit Room for nothing. The waitress lady was probably in the back somewhere calling the police on me right now. It was only a matter of time before Mama found out I was missing and sent Daddy out looking for me. It was only a matter of time before he found out about my mission, about where I'd gone and stopped caring enough to keep looking.

Get up! Go back out that door, get Artie's bike, and speed pump away.

I stood up.

"Where you going?" the auntie voice inquired.

I sat back down.

The waitress lady stood there holding a tray. She sat a plate in front of me with two biscuits on it, some butter, and three different kinds of jelly. Next came a tall, shimmering glass of milk. I tried to turn it down, but she said it was complimentary. She handed me a warm, soapy washcloth. "For your hands and face," she said. Until then I hadn't thought about how bad I must have looked and smelled after stepping in slime holes and rolling around on the ground tussling with the Devil Dog. I took the cloth and did the best I could with it.

The hostess sat down across from me. Placing her elbow on the table, she rested her chin on her fist and watched me as I ate. "So you one'a Big Josh's babies," she said.

I nodded.

"Who is your mother, honey?"

With those words, the milk curdled on my stomach and the biscuit turned to uncooked dough in my mouth.

"My mother . . . ?"

"Yes, sugar, your mother."

The dough started to swell. I couldn't swallow, I couldn't spit it out, and I dared not utter Mama's name.

"Frieda," the waitress lady said. "You can call me Miss Frieda."

Another waitress was passing our table. Miss Frieda touched her arm and the waitress stopped.

"Shirley," Miss Frieda said, "this child here's out on the street all times of night; wouldn't you want to know who her mother is?"

"I surely would," Miss Shirley said. "I'd want'a know who her mother is, and where she at so I could go give her a piece of my mind for not looking after her child no better."

"That's what um talkin 'bout," Miss Freida said. "That's what um talkin 'bout."

"I don't have one." I dropped my head out of shame for that lie.

Miss Frieda said, "I figured as much. Then you must not have a grandmama either, or auntie, or big sister 'cause no self-respecting woman would let a little girl out on these streets at night like this."

"How did you know?"

Miss Frieda called Shirley back. "This child wants to know how I know what a woman will do to care for a child, even if the child isn't her flesh and blood."

"To begin with, stand on her feet all day, turn around and work the night shift," Shirley said.

"Amen," said Miss Frieda. "And that's just to begin with."

"I meant, how'd you know I wasn't a boy?"

Miss Frieda put on a thoughtful look. "Well," she said, "I thought you were a boy when you first walked in—the clothes and cap and everything—and oh, the voice. Yes ma'am, you had me fooled. But after I had a good look at you, I saw you were just too pretty to be a boy."

Grown folks must think every kid they meet is a fool.

CHAPTER 17

"Hey there, Punkin."

I looked up into the smiling face of a movie star. She was Lena Horne, Eartha Kitt, and Diana Carroll all rolled up into one. From her pageboy, her perfectly arched brows, her blood red nails, to her two-piece, mint green, mohair boucle knit suit, she was it—and I hoped, my Christmas future.

"I know it's been a long time since we've seen one another, but aren't you gonna give me some sugar?"

I stood up, walked into her outstretched arms and sank into the hug she had waiting for me. I didn't know who she was, but in that moment I wasn't turning down hugs.

"Quit acting like you don't know me. After all, you must have been at least six months old the last time we sat down for a really good talk."

I liked her, even though I knew for sure I had never seen her before. "Who are you?"

She thanked Miss Frieda for calling her before answering. Frieda left and the beautiful woman turned to me. "My name is Juanita. I'm Josh's woman."

She sat down at the table, took out a cigarette, lit it, and didn't turn her head to exhale the smoke. "Where's Alex and . . . and . . . Vonnetta?"

"Vondra," I said.

She took another drag on her cigarette said, "Oh yes, that's right. Wanda."

Then she asked the same question Miss Frieda had. "Why you

118

running 'round by yourself, at night down here on Seventh Street?"

I leaned in toward her and lowered my voice. "I need to talk to Big Josh," I said. Then I told her about Jessie Mae. I told her what the sheik was doing to her, and how none of the grown folks did anything about it, and how useless her mother was, and how I needed $31.52 to buy a bus ticket back to Mississippi for her. I didn't know I was crying until Juanita handed me a napkin and said, "Wipe your eyes, baby."

Juanita looked at me and calmly changed the subject.

"So, your mama told you Josh is your daddy?"

"No," I said. "And if she found out I know she would be real mad."

"So why do you think Josh is your daddy?"

"My sister told me," I lied.

Juanita said, "Baby, I'm going to be honest with you. Josh is off somewhere doing his best to lose this month's rent in somebody's crap game.

She reached into her bosom and pulled out a twenty-dollar bill. "Take this. It should help some. I'll try to find Josh and see what he has left."

I took it and thanked her. It was warm, and it smelled like her, like roses and cinnamon. I didn't want to put it away. I wanted to press it against my face and hold it there until the roses and cinnamon faded. Still, I folded it into a tight little package and pushed it deep into my pants pocket.

Juanita stood up. "Now, let me get you home."

I told her I rode my friend's bike and showed it to her, leaning against the light pole. Juanita shook her head and told me to wait while she went to get the car. She retuned behind the wheel of a new copper-colored Cadillac with a chocolate-colored top made out of something that looked like leather. The bike fit in the trunk with room for a couple more.

"Okay, we're off to Chestnut Court"

I wasn't surprised that she knew where we lived. Too much had happened that night. I doubted I would ever be surprised by anything again. I sank down into the soft leather seat and tried to think through the mess I was in without simply giving in to a great big Chantelle-type snot fest. I was in trouble so big, just thinking about it made me lose my breath. I had risked everything and came up with half of nothing. Twenty dollars was a lot of money, but it wouldn't get Jessie Mae home.

Juanita tried to get me to talk, asking what I wanted for Christmas and stuff like that. I told her I wanted a bike. She asked me what Chantelle wanted. I told her about the baby, and she said, "Holy shit!" Then she said, "Excuse my French." She asked how Mama was and how she was taking the baby thing. I said Mama was fine. She pressed me for details, and I repeated, "Mama is fine," like I had been hypnotized to say that and nothing else.

The whole time I was thinking about how I had messed up everything, how the Jessie Mae in my dream had been right. So far nothing had gone the way it should have, and I knew that getting back in the house without anybody getting caught wouldn't go any better.

Juanita stomped on the brakes and made a sharp turn onto Union Street. She pulled up to the curb and turned off the engine. She turned to me. "Let me see what you've done to your hair." I tried to scramble out of her reach, but she yanked off my cap before I could. When she saw my boy cut, she said, "Poor baby." She ran her fingers through my hair and twisted a little of it into a curl. Then she said, "See that house with all the lights on? Somebody there owes me some money. I'm going to go collect it. You stay here. Okay? I want you to lay down in the backseat and cover up with that blanket back there. Cover your head, too, so nobody will know you're there. I'll be right back."

When she left I was glad that I was alone in the backseat covered up like something dead. I deserved it. And I needed to cry in peace.

Juanita got back sooner than I expected. I wiped my eyes on the blanket and sat up when I heard her get in and start the car. She let it idle while she opened the glove compartment, got a package of Doublemint out, and put two sticks in her mouth. Then she combed her hair and put on more lipstick.

When she finished, she said, "You can come back up here now."

"That's alright," I said."

Juanita snatched the blanket from my grip. "Get your butt up here!"

I crawled over the seat to the front.

"Here," she said and handed me two ten-dollar bills. "Now you have enough; I'm handing you off to your mama and daddy.

I pleaded with her. I bargained. I even begged, but Juanita was made of stone.

"I don't care, Punkin. I'm not leaving until I hand you off to somebody grown. I'd be the last person to try to say anything to you about running the streets, and I admire you for what you're trying to do for that little girl, but this is where you and me gone have a parting of ways if you think I'm going to let you out and just drive away.

Parking behind the Counts Boys' hippie van, across the street from our entrance, Juanita got out of the car and just about dragged me to our door. She wouldn't let me use Chantelle's key, either. She insisted on knocking, and she did hard and loud. When nobody answered immediately, she knocked even harder. Finally Daddy shouted, "Who is it?" She answered, Juanita Steckly, like everyone knew who she was.

Daddy flung open the door. Mama stood behind him, clutching my severed braids, and behind her stood Chantelle, looking like somebody on the radio had just announced the world was ending in ten minutes.

CHAPTER 18

Daddy squinted at me like his eyesight had suddenly gone bad.

Until that moment, when he saw me standing in the doorway, I don't think it had sunk in that I was not in my room, snugly tucked away, in my bed next to Chantelle's.

"Bernie?" he asked, his voice so soft it seemed he was talking to himself.

Juanita said, "May I?" Daddy stood back and she stepped through the door dragging me in with her.

"I found her down at Esther's Orbit Room looking for Josh."

"Looking for Josh?" Daddy asked as though that was the most incredible thing he had ever heard.

He turned to stare at Mama, she whirled around to glare at Chantelle who stood there shaking her head.

"Not me. Not me. I didn't tell her anything. Honest."

"She smelling herself," Mama announced. "That's all. Thinks she's grown. Thinks she can take a page from Chantelle's book and run buck wild."

Daddy got down on one knee in front of me like he was proposing. He said, "Why, baby girl?"

I was so ashamed of hurting him, I couldn't speak.

Juanita wasn't worried about hurting anybody's feelings.

"I didn't bother explaining the distribution of daddies in you all's li'l family," she said. "Figured that was something you all would want to handle. I just want to say one thing, though, while I'm on the subject and that is this: It's not right for a child to grow up not knowing who her people are. I don't care who's paying the bills."

"Alex's Bernadine's daddy," Mama said with a tone that said "we've gone over this before, and I'm getting sick of repeating myself."

"I'm not talking about Bernadine."

Daddy was standing up now looking from Mama to Juanita.

"Daddy's my daddy," Chantelle whispered to no one in particular.

Then it happened. The piano crashed down out of the sky smack dab on top of my head. Fireworks exploded, birds tweeted, and a light bulb lit up.

I had gotten it all wrong. Chantelle had tried to tell me, but I thought she was dumb and I hadn't listened. Miss Donna had tried to tell me, but I thought she was lying and still I didn't listen. I wondered if even li'l Maxine had tried to tell me.

I leaped into Daddy's arms and squeezed him so tight he squeaked. Daddy looked me in the eyes and nodded. I turned to Chantelle and said, "I'm sorry." And I really was. I was Daddy's girl. He was *my* real daddy, but not hers.

Daddy drew Chantelle to him and put an arm around her shoulders.

"Nobody's got any reason to be sorry," he said. "These are my girls. I'm their daddy, and that's all there is to it."

He looked dead at Juanita when he said that.

Juanita shrugged but she didn't look away.

Mama lashed at me with my discarded braids. "Your hair," she wailed, "all your beautiful hair. Gone. Just look at you. You look like some ashy-assed Ubangi!"

"No man has ever asked me for some hair," Juanita said with a hint of a smile that suggested how wicked she could be if she wanted to.

That broke the tension, at least for Daddy. He laughed out loud. "The Divine One—Miss Sarah Vaughn, or was that The Queen—Miss Dinah Washington?"

"Take your pick," Juanita said.

Mama opened the front door. "Thank you for dropping Bernadine off," she said looking pointedly at Juanita.

Juanita said, "I'm not done." She took a seat on the couch without it being offered, leaned back, and crossed her legs. She took a pack of cigarettes from her purse and lit one.

Mama said, "I don't allow smoking in here."

Juanita said, "It's your house," and snuffed out the cigarette on the sole of her shoe and put it in her pocket.

"Getting back to your original question, Alex," she said. "It's my understanding that Bernie was trying to get help for a little girl whose mama been letting her ol' man rape her."

Mama turned the radio up loud when the Sheik was messing with Jessie Mae. Chantelle read the Bible—I don't have to tell you which parts. Daddy beat up the Sheik. But until Juanita, nobody had said the word. And the word was rape.

"I don't appreciate you coming to my house with your gutter ways and using gutter language," Mama said.

Juanita shrugged and said, "The truth is the light."

"What goes on upstairs is not Bernadine's business."

"But Mama, her bedroom is right above mine."

A look of understanding slowly worked its way across Mama's face.

Daddy hugged me and said, "Walls like tissue paper . . . I'm so sorry, baby."

Chantelle said, "What about me? We share the same room."

Juanita looked at her and said, "Let well enough be, honey."

"That's why you ought to stay out of grown folks' business," Mama said to me. "We got Jessie Mae out of there."

"When you say we who are you talking about?" Daddy asked. "And when did all of this happen?"

"We women. This afternoon while the kids were at school. She came out to go to the washhouse, and we grabbed her, took her to Donna's house, washed her up, put her in some decent clothes, and fed her."

"She still there?" I asked. Please, Mama, can I go see her."

Mama shook her head. "She wouldn't stay. Said her mama was sick, and she couldn't leave her. We said we would go get her mother, too. But she waited until Donna's back was turned and sneaked back up there."

"Seems to me," Juanita said, "we have a classic case of too little too late."

Mama said, "We did our best."

Juanita acted like Mama hadn't said a word.

She said, "I never did believe in sneaking round, going through back doors and shit. If you all will excuse me, I'm going to retrieve something from my car, and when I get back, I'm going in through the front door to see about that child."

Juanita left and Daddy went to the bedroom to throw on a jacket over his pajamas. He was waiting for Juanita in the stairwell when she returned. I was pretty sure he had his gun. Mama didn't say a word. She just pursed her lips and shook her head.

According to Daddy, the door to the apartment was standing open, and all the lights were on. He had hesitated, but Juanita walked in like she owned the place. She looked in rooms, and under beds. She opened closets and cabinets, and checked everything.

"Didn't seem like they packed much," Juanita said. "Then again, maybe they didn't have that much to pack in the first place."

Mama said, "Well, we did our best."

"Speaking of such, I need to talk to you in private," Juanita said.

Mother said, "Whatever you have to say to me you can say in front of my husband."

"Suit yourself. We need to talk about Chantelle."

Mama realized she had made a mistake and tried to stop Juanita, but it was too late. Daddy wanted to hear what she had to say too. He said, "Go on Juanita, if you don't mind."

Juanita said, "Josh may have his faults—I'd be the first one to admit that—he does, though, love his child and he tries to do right by her. That little bit of support he's been paying isn't much but at least it's something. I don't think he's going to be happy when he finds out you let his baby girl get pregnant, to say nothing about how I found your other little girl, wandering around on Seventh Street by herself at night." Having had her say, Juanita got up and left.

I read somewhere that after they dropped the bomb on Hiroshima in Japan there was a kind of silence nobody had ever heard before. That kind of silence invaded our living room.

Daddy was slowly swelling up with anger while Mama was shrinking like the witch in The Wizard of Oz.

"So, you been seeing him behind my back, taking his money. What else you been doing?"

"Baby, listen. I haven't been *seeing* him. From time to time Juanita drops off a little change, nothing much. I use it to send the girls to the movies or something. I don't even tell them where it came from."

"Behind my back, Vondra. Behind my back!"

"Baby, please . . . I'm sorry."

"This is my family. I take care of my family, my girls. That Negro has never done anything worthwhile in his life. I work hard, I struggle, I just about kiss the white man's ass for you and these girls, and this is the thanks I get. You promised me, Vondra. You promised."

"I haven't seen him. The girls didn't even know who he was until Donna got to running her mouth."

Daddy dropped down on the couch and cradled his head in his arms. His shoulders shook. Me and Chantelle teared up. I sat down next to him.

"Daddy, I'm sorry. Honest, Daddy, I'm so sorry. It was Jessie Mae. I just had to do something to help her get home to her grandmother. I tried everything, Daddy. I didn't want to have anything to do with Big Josh. He was my last resort."

Chantelle said, "I'm sorry too, Daddy."

Daddy looked up and said, "Now, what have you got to be sorry about?"

"Chantelle lowered her head and said, "You know . . ."

I said, "Daddy, listen to me. You don't have to be jealous of Big Josh."

"Who's jealous?" Daddy said real quick.

Mama left the room and came back with the extension cord.

Daddy said, "Put it down, Vondra."

Mama said, "Now, see, that's what's wrong. You spoil them, then you always so hurt when they act like fools. I'm the only one who's trying to teach them some sense. Bernadine knows she's got a whuppin coming." Mama turned to me. "What you doing, Bernadine? Trying to break up me and your daddy?"

I said "No, Mama," and stood up to take my beating.

Daddy said, "Sit down, Bernadine." Then he said to Mama, "Ain't going be anymore beating these girls like they're animals."

"That's what you say now, but wait until Bernadine comes up pregnant."

Daddy sprung from the couch and had raised his hand to hit Mama before he caught himself. They stood there in each other's face, breathing hard, staring one another down. Mama broke first. She turned and stomped off to the kitchen. Daddy went to the bedroom and slammed the door. Mama was so angry, she had to beat something, so she whupped the refrigerator with the extension cord for about ten minutes.

Chantelle said, "See, that could'a been you."

I shivered. I was glad Daddy had laid down the law about the whuppins because I didn't know how long I could live a life whose sole purpose was to avoid getting beat.

I asked Chantelle what really happened to Jessie Mae but she didn't know.

I told her I had seen Cut'n Ollie.

"How is he?" She asked.

"His booty was all hanging out."

Chantelle laughed and said, "It figures."

I didn't laugh because it was kind of sad. "I think we better tell Daddy so he can go see about him."

Chantelle said, "What did Tonto say to the Lone Ranger?"

I punched her arm.

"So, what else did you do?" Chantelle wanted to know. "How'd you get all those scratches and bruises an' stuff? Did you see Big Josh?"

I said, "Maybe we should go to the bedroom and talk."

"Maybe you should go to the bathroom and get reacquainted with some soap and water, first. Save a sister a headache."

I took her suggestion. Mama was bunked down on the couch when I came out of the bathroom. She glared at me, but she didn't say a word when I walked by. Chantelle had fallen asleep. The *body* that I had made out of old clothes was still in my bed under the covers like I'd left it, but somebody, probably Mama, had decapitated it. I didn't bother removing it. I put on my gown and climbed in next to it.

Jessie Mae was gone. Her mama was gone. And so was the Sheik, but who gave a care about him. Nobody knew when they had left or where they went.

I dreamed about Jessie Mae every single night until they found her.

After work the next day, Daddy took me with him to the barbershop. His process needed redoing, but he had it cut off, all the way down to the naps. The barber took a pick that looked almost like a wide fork and picked out all his hair until it was standing up on his head. Next the barber took his long, skinny barber scissors and shaped Daddy's hair into a perfectly round dandelion-do like Brother Calley's, only smaller.

"What you think, baby girl?" Daddy asked.

"Oh Daddy, you are so fine!" I said.

The barbershop erupted into laughter, but I didn't mind. My daddy was looking good.

"Okay, your turn."

"For what?"

"Your Afro. You can't go around looking like Cut'n Ollie the rest of your life."

I climbed into the barber's chair. He picked out my hair, and then he spent the next hour shaping it with his long skinny scissors. When he finished and held up a mirror for me to see what he'd done, I was so surprised I couldn't speak.

Daddy said, "Well?"

"Beautiful," was all I could get out. "Beautiful."

CHAPTER 19

The shoe washed up on the rocks under one of the docks in Fruit Town.

Some boys found it, BJ Simmons, Leandus, and the rest of them. They had been hunting for dead seagulls or maybe the carcass of a big ol' wharf rat like the one they found the last time. All they found this time, though, was the shoe with the run-down heel and a hole that had been cut to give room to the baby toe. But the boys were not disappointed. They courted with the shoe, sticking it in the face of one little West Oakland beauty after another. The odor alone sent the girls running and screaming.

Connie Ruth was the prettiest girl at Thompkins Elementary School. She was also the only girl in the entire school who could hit one of Mr. Echo's fastballs. Connie Ruth loved her some BJ Simmons. She wrote "Miz BJ Simmons" all over her book covers. But it wasn't true love, because when BJ Simmons stuck that stinky shoe in her face she didn't run. She wished she had run instead of punching BJ in the stomach so hard he threw up the Cheerios he'd had for breakfast along with something that looked like raw egg.

Connie Ruth told Moochie about the shoe, Moochie told Niecy, Niecy told Andrea, and Andrea told me. I had to see the shoe for myself. At the first recess, I waited outside the boy's restroom until BJ Simmons came out.

"What you doing hanging round here?" BJ asked. He was so used to girls, grown women, and even some men telling him how good looking he was that he acted like he already knew my answer would be, "I was waiting for you, BJ."

"Let me see the shoe."

BJ's boys gathered around him.

"What shoe?" BJ said, all innocent like.

"The shoe, BJ. The one you found in Fruit Town." I was trembling. BJ thought it was from passion. I was scared the shoe would be hers.

One of his boys held the shoe over his head. "You mean this one?"

I turned to him, and he tossed it to another boy. I didn't bother running from one boy to another like a cute girl getting teased would have. Instead, I grabbed BJ by the collar of his jacket, and snatched him to me. He was so shocked he didn't resist.

"I want the shoe," I said.

"Hey man, give this crazy broad the shoe."

The boy tossed it to me. I caught the black-and-white saddle oxford, with the hole cut over the baby toe, and cradled it in my arms. I dropped to my knees cradling that shoe. Then I sat down on the damp grass and wept.

I'm sorry, Jessie Mae. I'm so sorry. I tried but I messed up. I'm sorry.

The bell rang and everyone went back to class. I didn't bother moving. I couldn't move until Jessie Mae knew how sorry I was.

I could see people inside the classrooms gathered at the windows, gawking at me, but I didn't care, and I didn't move.

Somebody told Mr. Zimmerman and he came out to where I was. Shaking with the palsy, he carefully picked his way across the damp grass. He wasn't happy when he got to where I was.

"Young lady," he said, "you get up this very minute or you're in for some very big trouble." I rocked Jessie Mae's shoe and tried to explain, but he didn't believe me or he just plain didn't care.

"Are you getting up or will I be forced to make a call?" I wasn't getting up, and didn't care who he called, and I told him so. He picked his way back across the lawn to call my parents or the loony bin, or whatever.

When the principal left, the Negro lunch lady came out and sat down on the damp grass next to me. "What's the matter, baby?" She asked. And I leaned against her shoulder and told her about Jessie Mae and her sorry mama and the Sheik and how I tried to save Jessie Mae but messed up. I cried all over her lunch lady uniform and got snot and stuff on it but she didn't mind.

She called the police and made a report. They took the shoe.

Jessie Mae's body washed up two days later in Fruit Town.

Trying not to think about all the ways I had messed up, all the ways I let Jessie Mae down, wore me down. Guilt rode me to the point of exhaustion. It sent me to bed and pinned me there. I did not have the strength to go to school. There were only a few more days left before Christmas holiday so Mama didn't make me go.

Most evenings Daddy came home to find me and Chantelle in bed, Mama on the couch, dirty dishes in the sink, and the house engulfed in so much funk it seemed it might be flammable. At first he complained about having to work two jobs—one at work and one at home. But Mama said that was what she had done all these years and when did he ever hear her complain. After that he stopped complaining and just did his best to keep up with everything— cooking, cleaning, and washing clothes. He liked to cook weird stuff like macaroni with sardines. His specialty, though was pancakes. He cooked them every other night. At first I ate the pancakes. But, after a while, opening and closing my mouth to make my jaws chew overwhelmed me with exhaustion, so I stopped trying. Chantelle said if I didn't start back to eating, I had no chance of growing any kind of titties, whatsoever. By then I didn't care. Jessie Mae was dead and that was all that mattered.

I thought about the Sheik a lot. I daydreamed about killing him, but I knew even if I got the chance, even if somebody tied him up and handed me a loaded gun, I probably wouldn't be able to pull the trigger. I would have to find someone to do it for me. Each thought about the Sheik sapped a bit more of my strength. In the back of my mind I knew if I didn't stop thinking about him I would never be able to get out of bed again, never be able to stand up straight again, never be able to walk.

After a while I stopped getting up in the middle of the night and squeezing in next to Mama on the couch. I stopped getting out of bed at all except to go to the bathroom. Later I stopped doing even that. Daddy's reaction was to call me Punkin and every sweet name he could think of and to cook more pancakes. He cooked pancakes until Mama and Chantelle begged him to stop. It seemed like in some strange way Mama and Daddy's appetites got all tangled up in mine, and they stopped eating, too. Daddy started smoking again, and he seemed to live off cigarettes. I think Mama was living off black coffee.

Mama coached Daddy on what to bring home to tempt me to eat. "Why don't you pick up a pint of black walnut ice cream?" she'd say. Or "How 'bout some of that barbecue you got down by the train station that time?" Daddy brought home French fries from Quickways, rib-tip sandwiches from Ella's Smoke House, and pound cake from Neldam's Bakery. Miss Bea even baked a jelly cake and sent it over. By this time nobody but Chantelle was eating. Any and everything that came through the door went straight down her gullet only to be puked up again. In just one day, she finished off half of Miss Bea's jelly cake. Mama threw the rest of it down the garbage chute when she found out.

Mama called Chantelle's puking, "morning sickness," but Chantelle couldn't keep anything down morning, noon, or night. That didn't stop her from eating, through. She scarfed down everything she could get her hands on, only to throw it up before it could do her or the baby

133

much good.

When Chantelle wasn't puking all over everything, she had her booty in my face and her head stuck out the window gossiping with all kinds of folks—Artie and James, Maxine and Sherry, Brother Calley and the Grove Street College Boys, even Miss Viola—everybody except Charlesetta. Her mother wouldn't let her hang around with Chantelle anymore, because "it was a proven fact" that Chantelle was a bad influence, and that she was "so fast, she went out and got messed up." The following year, when Charlesetta got pregnant, her mother said it was all Chantelle's fault.

Ol' Bad Richard came by almost every night. Late at night, he stood beneath the window, looking up at Chantelle, and talking for hours. Because he still refused to go to school, his grandmother kicked him out, and now he was living in abandoned houses in our old neighborhood. Chantelle sneaked food to him. She gave him all of our money, including the forty-three dollars I had raised to rescue Jessie Mae. In exchange, he told her all kinds of stories about living life as a kid hobo.

"See if you can find my cousin Cut'n Ollie and his son Reno. They were living in our old house. Bernadine's worried about them. She said the last time she saw Cut'n Ollie his booty was hanging out."

They both had a good giggle about that.

"What does it look like?" asked Ol' Bad Richard.

"Skinny, flat, yellow, wino booty."

"I'll keep my eyes open."

The next night, just before daybreak, Ol' Bad Richard slung a handful of pebbles at the window. I had to wake Chantelle.

I could hear Ol' Bad Richard's feet moving like he was dancing. His chains were jangling. Before Chantelle had the window all the way open, he blurted, "Guess what, guess what! I saw your Cut'n Ollie and Reno. They fine except Cut'n Ollie was walking with a cane—well not exactly a cane—more like a tree limb he trimmed the leaves off. They still staying at your old house."

Chantelle turned to me. "You hear that, Nae-Nae? Cut'n Ollie is just fine."

Even Chantelle had taken to calling me baby names. I didn't respond.

Then Ol' Bad Richard said something that made me bolt upright in my bed. "Guess who else I saw. I saw the—"

Chantelle cut him off.

"Don't be coming 'round here talking that mess. She'll be howling in her sleep again."

But Ol' Bad Richard was too excited to stop there. "You ain't gon' believe where he's crashing!"

Chantelle slammed the window shut. But I heard what he said anyway.

That evening, when Daddy came home from work, he peeked in to see how I was doing. He found me staring at the wall, as I picked through my broken thoughts to piece together a plan.

"Brought you some peanut brittle, Punkin."

The hope in Daddy's voice made me sad enough to cry. But I didn't. I had to be strong enough to hold on until I worked everything out. I didn't allow myself to blink. I had to focus, or everything I'd stacked up in my mind would come crashing down, again. Daddy stood there, waiting for me to be glad he bought me some candy. Finally, after I had everything worked out, I turned away and pulled the covers over my head.

Daddy nudged me. "You're acting rather *reticent* today."

I didn't go for the okey doke.

But, Daddy didn't leave. Instead, he peeled back my covers like my bed was a can of sardines. "Come on, baby girl. Sit up here and talk to your daddy."

He helped me sit up, handling me with the kind of gentleness you use with a baby or somebody who is old and all broken down.

"Punkin," he whispered, "I want you to tell me something. Okay?"

He took a deep breath and turned away. "Did Willie do anything to you when he had you up there locked in that cage?"

I had promised Mama I would never let Daddy find out about me getting trapped in the Sheik's cage, but he knew anyway. Now he was asking me a question I didn't have the strength to answer. I wanted to pull the covers back over my head and stay like that for a thousand years. Daddy turned to me so he could look me in the eye. I dropped back down on the bed and pulled the quilt over my head.

"You can tell me, baby girl."

But he shouldn't have insisted on an answer. He should have known he couldn't trust my truth, that mine tasted different on the tongue than his. I could have said the Sheik hadn't done anything to me, but would Daddy have believed that? Would he have thought I was just too ashamed to admit the horrible truth? As a matter of fact, the Sheik had done something to me, something far worse than anything Daddy could have imagined. The Sheik had forced me to bear witness to his destruction of a girl. He had forced me to watch, forced me to listen as he handled her the way a bad kid handles a moth—pulling off one wing and then the other, before smashing the life out of it, and walking away. The Sheik had shown me how little a girl can matter and, in the process, he had shown me how little I mattered. Only a blood red lie would free me from that knowledge, release me from my bed, and allow me to eat again. And that lie could be told only by silence. So I didn't say anything. And that gave me power, way more power than I ever had, more power even than when I was slinging the bike chain.

My silence said, "He touched me, Daddy. He did nasty things to me." I heard Daddy sob. He tried to uncover my head, but I clung to the quilt and wouldn't let him. He sat there on the edge of my bed for a while, and then he gave up and left the room.

"You should'a told him," Chantelle said.

I stuck my arm from under the quilt and flipped her off.

"You should'a told him that the Sheik didn't mess with you," she insisted.

I snatched the quilt off my head and sat up. I reached over and got a pencil and paper from the nightstand between our beds. I wrote in big capital letters: "WILL YOU KILL THE SHIEK FOR ME?" Then I drew two boxes and wrote "Yes" under one and "No" under the other. I put an asterisk next to the "No." At the bottom of the page I put another asterisk and next to it I wrote: "Then shut the fuck up!" I folded it neatly in half and handed it to Chantelle. She read it and snorted. She wadded the paper into a tight ball and threw it at me.

"You know you crazy," she said. "Mama and Daddy ought'a put you in the crazy house over at Napa, and collect their seventy-five dollars."

CHAPTER 20

Over the days, Daddy grew quieter. Chantelle said he spent most nights sitting in the dark, staring at the red glow of his cigarette, sometimes letting it burn all the way down to his finger tips. He took to doing the hundred-mile march after he finished the evening chores, although it was more like 7,962 miles most nights. I could hear him outside my door going back and forth. Back and forth. Every couple of hours he'd step outside to get some air. If you looked down from our bedroom window, you could just make him out, standing at the edge of the entryway. Sometimes people came by to talk to him. He stood listening in silence, the tip of his cigarette glowing and then fading.

I caught snatches of Mama and Daddy arguing just about every night. It wasn't the loud kind with Mama slamming doors and Daddy turning the TV volume up real high to show he was ignoring her. These fights were different. They came in short bursts of sharp-edged whispers followed by long blank spaces of silence. Daddy wanted to go out; Mama didn't want him to. One night Mama blocked the door so Daddy couldn't leave. The next night when she tried that he picked her up and moved her out of the way.

"Put me down, Alex!"

I uncovered my head and sat up to hear better.

" . . . her mother, Alex. I ought to know."

"You didn't know about Chantelle."

"So now it's my fault Chantelle is fast?"

"You the one talking about knowing so much."

"I know this—you may end up in San Quentin over somebody

who isn't even worth it."

"You saying that little girl in there all balled up in her bed isn't worth it?"

"You know what I mean. *He* isn't worth it."

"I gotta be able to live with myself, Vonnie. I gotta be able to look my child in the eye without feeling shame 'cause I didn't protect her."

"I'm telling you, Alex, he didn't touch her. But you go on. Do what you have to do. I can't stop you. I just want you to know this isn't you. You're not a killer."

I heard the front door open and close. I curled down under my covers to wait for Daddy to do the deed for me. The next thing I knew, Mama had stomped into our room and snatched off my covers.

"Get up," she snapped. "You got your Daddy all riled up—get your li'l ass up."

I grabbed at the covers. She snatched them completely off the bed and flung them to the floor. Hands on her hips, Mama stood there glowering at me, daring me to stay in bed a second longer. I turned on my side and forced myself to a sitting position. My head felt like a balloon full of helium, my neck like the string connecting it to my body. I stared to wobble, but a look from Mama helped me steady myself. I eased one leg over the bed, rested, and was about to ease the other one over when Mama grabbed my foot and flung it to the floor. She grabbed me by my upper arms and jerked me up. For a moment the floor and ceiling seemed to be playing tag. My stomach lurched. I would have thrown up but it was empty.

"Stand your ass up!"

Chantelle leaped out of bed and wrapped her arms around me.

"Mama, she sick!"

I tried to stand, but my back didn't seem to have any bone. I slumped full body against Chantelle.

"I don't care. She's getting her behind up, and she's taking a

139

bath."

With Chantelle's help, I took a step toward the door. I grabbed the corner of the dresser to steady myself.

"Straighten up and walk. There are no cripples in this house."

Mama stood back as Chantelle and I squeezed past her to the door. "I told you what would happen if your Daddy found out about you getting caught in that cage."

I turned around to face her.

"But, Mama, I didn't say a word."

"That's right, Bernadine. You didn't say a word. You let your daddy walk out of here thinking the Sheik put his hands on you."

Chantelle helped me with my bath, scrubbing my back and getting all the toe jam from between my toes. Then she helped dry me off. I was surprised how good it felt to have someone take care me. I had forgotten what it felt like to have a big sister, what it felt like not to be all alone in the world. But every time I thought about something good, like having a big sister again, I thought about something bad, like failing poor Jessie Mae. After my bath, I had to drink some of Mama's nasty tea that's supposed to cure everything. Then Mama set about growing my hair back. I sat between her knees as she greased my scalp with Dixie Peach and Glover's Mange mixed together and pinched my hair up into a couple hundred little braids. They were so tight it felt like my scalp was separating from my skull.

Funny thing is I felt better after the bath and everything. I felt good enough to get some paper and sit down to write a letter.

Dear Miz Alice Louise Bing:

It is with a heavy heart that I am writing to you. I am truly sorry to have to tell you that your beloved granddaughter, Jessie Mae, is dead. It pains me to tell you that she perished in the icy waters off Jack London Square here in Oakland, California.

Jessie Mae was a good child, and she always tried to help her mother. I regret to tell you, however, that your daughter, Lee Ann, was a sorry excuse for a mother. She let a man called Willie Nathan, who she lived with, mistreat Jessie Mae and do nasty things to her. I am certain he killed her.

I tried to help Jessie Mae, but I am just a kid and nobody took me seriously. If you would like to seek vengeance on the man who murdered your beloved granddaughter, Jessie Mae, please let me know and I will help you. I know where to find him. He lives in an old abandoned house. My cousin, Oliver Washington, knows which one.

Sincerely,

Bernadine Mattocks

P.S. I read the Bible all the time, and it says vengeance is okay.

We heard Daddy coming up the stairs. Usually he came up so quickly it sounded like he was tap dancing. This time he was going slowly like he was carrying something heavy and he had to stop and rest, every so often.

Mama waited for him at our opened door. "You find him?" she whispered.

Daddy shook his head. I have never seen Mama wilt like that before. Daddy pulled her to him and she rested her head on his shoulder. Mama held on to Daddy like he was her life raft, and he held on to her like she was his.

Daddy looked over the top of Mama's head and saw me sitting on the couch, scrubbed clean, Vaselined down, hair pinched up into hundreds of little braids.

"Well, look who's up."

"Daddy, I'm really worried about Cut'n Ollie." I don't know how I managed to squeeze out enough tears to have them run down my face.

"You want me to go see about him, baby girl?"

I did not trust myself to speak, so I nodded. I nodded to Daddy's question and to the voice inside my head screaming at me: *Are you crazy? You gon' send your own daddy out to kill a man? You are one sorry, pathetic, ugly, no-haired, li'l ho!* I already knew everything the voice was saying, so I nodded again.

Mama was helping Daddy out of his coat. "Your daddy's not going anywhere tonight. Ollie's been a wino all this time. He knows how to take care of himself. If he doesn't, he picked the wrong occupation."

Daddy looked at me over Mama's head and winked.

CHAPTER 21

Who would have thought Miss Donna's little Maxine had been right all along about the daddy of Chantelle's baby. Well, kinda right. At least she put the baby in the right family, although Miss Calley definitely wasn't the daddy.

One Sunday, Miss Calley—still in her church clothes—and her son, Brother Calley, the Grove Street College Boy, paid us a visit. Miss Calley carried an offering of freshly baked monkey bread, and Brother Calley lugged a big box.

"Brother and Sister Mattock, I have something to discuss with you of great import," Miss Calley said. "Would you mind asking Chantelle to join us?"

Daddy's jaws got tight. Chantelle came out. She was all dressed up and had done her hair. She sat down next to the Grove Street College Boy, and he put his arm around her. Daddy and Mama both glared at him, and he sheepishly took his arm back.

Miss Calley continued, "We are an honorable family. My husband, rest his soul, and I tried to raise our children with a sense of decency. However, young people have a way of occasionally straying from the paved path."

Miss Calley was a deaconess at her church, and she loved to talk when the deacons would let her, which looked like it wasn't often enough. Daddy was getting impatient, and Mama was doing a slow burn.

Daddy looked straight at the Brother Calley and said, "You have something you want to say to me, *brother*?"

Miss Calley looked flustered—she had not finished her beautiful speech. Brother Calley swallowed and said, "Yes, sir. I would like your permission to marry your daughter."

"You have some nerve, don't you? This is a child," Mama said pointing at Chantelle, who attempted to bristle but hadn't quite mastered the concept.

Daddy patted Mama's hand and she calmed a little. "Brother Calley, how old are you?"

"Nineteen, sir."

"And how old do you think my daughter is?"

"Sixteen."

"That's still statutory," Mama interjected. Daddy patted her hand again.

"She's thirteen," Daddy said.

Brother Calley didn't seem surprised, but his mother was clearly scared. "Before we say some things that we may later regret, let me suggest that we take one another's hands, bow our heads, and ask the Lord for guidance."

Nobody moved. Daddy glared at Brother Calley, and Mama glared at his mother.

Daddy said, "Let's just get to the real issue. No, you can't marry my little girl. Yes, you will support your child."

Miss Calley tried to respond. "We have every intention—"

But Daddy cut her off. "Sister Calley, I'm speaking to the man here. The man who I am presuming knows what it means to take responsibility and to care for his own, the man who by all rights should be sitting his ass up in jail."

"Brother Mattock, I assure you I do know the meaning of responsibility. I will not let you down."

"You already have," Daddy said. "And one more thing—you ain't slick. I knew it was you even before my wife told me. I was just waiting to see if you had it in you to do the right thing."

Brother Calley didn't move. He kept his eyes locked on Daddy's. Everybody else turned to stare at Mama. She shrugged.

Chantelle leaped up and ran to our room. Poor thing, I guess she thought Mama and Daddy were going to let her get married before she'd even learned how to mop a floor, cook a pot of beans, or hem a skirt.

Daddy shook his head like he was trying to clear his thoughts. "Brother Calley—Norman—it's Norman, isn't it?

"Yes, sir."

"Norman, do you fish?"

Norman couldn't tell where the conversation was heading, but he answered, "Yes, sir."

"What's biting this time of year?"

"Crappies."

"Where, man? Where?"

"Over at Lake Berryessa. You want largemouth I recommend the Delta, up 'round Stockton."

"I could stand me a mess a crappies right about now. When the next time you going out?"

Norman didn't know.

Mama tried to say something, but Daddy raised his hand. "Why don't you go back to the room and relax," he said.

Mama looked at him, gave him a tiny nod, and left.

Daddy turned to Sister Calley. "Me and Norman got some fish tales to tell, and you know how it is when brothers get to lying." He patted her hands, which were still folded on the table in front of her. "Why don't you go on home now? But, I want you to know you are always welcome in this house."

You could tell by the way Sister Calley scooted her behind back and forth on the chair and shuffled her feet without actually getting up that she didn't want to leave.

145

Daddy winked at her and said, "I'm not going to hurt Ol' Norman."

Sister Calley scooted some more.

Daddy called Chantelle back to the room. Her eyes were red like she had been crying. She came and stood near me on the couch. I reached up and took her hand.

"Baby girl, why don't you walk Sister Calley home?"

Chantelle let go of my hand and took Sister Calley's. They left together.

Daddy said, "I gotta put on dinner. You cook, Norman?"

"No, Sir—"

"Son, call me *Alex*, call me man, call me *Pop* even. Call me anything but *sir*. Okay, Norman?"

Norman agreed. Daddy wrapped an arm around his shoulder.

"You like macaroni, man?"

Norman wasn't sure.

With his arm still locked around Norman's shoulder, Daddy walked him to the kitchen.

"I got this recipe that'll blow your mind."

Norman came over just about every day after that. Mama let him "keep company" with Chantelle, even though Chantelle was already pregnant. It seemed important to Mama that things be done in a certain order, even pretend things. At first they just sat on the couch together, looking embarrassed and barely talking. Then they started holding hands. When Chantelle threw up, Norman would hold her hair her back to keep the puke off of it, and then he would clean up after her.

I think Mama started liking him when she saw that. She liked that he wasn't "nice nasty." She like the way he scooped the puke up on newspaper and folded it in a tight little bundle, and then asked for baking soda to sprinkle over the nasty smelling spot to soak up the rest. She liked that he was always telling Chantelle to put her feet up or running back and forth to get her water or to change the channel on the TV or to get a magazine for her. He started calling Chantelle sweet names like "Li'l Mama" and "Baby Doll" and "Sugar." Chantelle was throwing up less and giggling more.

Norman christened me, "Li'l Sis," as in, "Scoot over, Sugar, and let *Li'l Sis* up here on the couch so she can watch *Ed Sullivan*, too." Bed was becoming less appealing when he was around, although according to Mama I was "still walking around like a hant."

Chantelle was spending more and more time over at Sister Calley's, learning how to boil a pot of beans, hem a skirt, and mix Carnation milk and Karo syrup together to make baby formula. Mama had been trying to teach her two of those things for years, but Sister Calley did it in just a few days.

Norman spent time with Daddy too—learning his secret recipes, helping him haul stuff and move people to earn extra money. They talked about everything and argued about most of it.

Daddy: "Hell, man, I read Marcuse too. I *recognize myself* in an empty plate after my child has eaten her fill . . . and when it's raining outside I look like a house with the heater on. Shit!"

Norman: "Nobody gives RL Burnside credit, man. As far as I'm concerned, he's the greatest bluesman ever, no lie."

Daddy: "I'll give you that but not for the reason you think. You know ol' RL did some time in the pen for killing a man. Know what he said about it? 'I didn't mean to kill nobody . . . I just meant to shoot the sonofabitch in the head. Him dying was between him and the Lord.' Now that's a bluesman."

You knew when they got quiet and leaned their heads in close to one another that they were talking about serious stuff. Once I walked in on them like that in the kitchen and I heard my name. Daddy looked so sad. I turned around and walked right back out. I didn't like the thought that my name could do that to him.

Sometimes they went out late at night and didn't come back until it was time for Daddy to go to work. I asked Daddy what they were doing out so late.

"Hunting" was what he said.

CHAPTER 22

Christmas had come and gone with us hardly noticing. We didn't get a tree or decorate anything, maybe because we didn't have anything to celebrate. It seemed we were settling into a new life as a completely different family, one that had a daddy who worked a whole bunch of jobs; a mama who lost her job for missing too many days and who stayed at home, mostly on the couch; one sister who puked all over everything; and another sister who dreamed, every night, about a dead girl.

The couch was still Mama's home base, but she had started doing more stuff around the house, like cooking and cleaning. It wasn't long before she decided it was time for me to do the same—not just get off the couch, but go back to school.

Daddy didn't agree.

"I don't think she's ready, baby. Look at those bags under her eyes. She still not steady on her feet."

Mama stood with her hands on her hips and stared down at me on the couch. She pressed her lips together and studied me, nodding like I confirmed something she'd known all along.

"Un huh, she's getting off her behind and going to school. I'm up, she gets up."

"But, baby, she's been through a lot."

"So have I."

There was no way Daddy could argue that point, and he was too smart to even try.

Mama continued to study me.

She said, "I'm not a fool, Bernadine."

I looked up to say, "What?" but Daddy beat me to it.

"Why you brow-beating the child, Vonnie?"

Mama looked at Daddy and sighed. The way she held her breath a beat longer than she should have and pulled her tight lips up under her nose, told me she was trying to decide whether she would tell Daddy whatever it was she knew.

I hurried and said, "I miss school, Mama. I want to go back."

Mama's eyes shot me a *Don't try to play me* warning.

Daddy said, "You don't have to go back until you're ready, Punkin." He was looking directly at Mama when he said it.

Hands on her hip, lips pinched to the side, Mama held her position. I could almost feel her thought waves: *Here we are, one child pregnant, the other one bald, half crazy, and so hell-bent on revenge she'll have you out on the streets doing who knows what before you even realize it. Once again, you fall for the ol' okey doke.*

Mama made sure she had Daddy's eye. Bending slightly from the waist and leaning in close to him, she said, "Men are such fools."

Chantelle was careful not to come out of the bedroom while Daddy and Mama where having their go-round about school. She wasn't going to school either. Partially because she hadn't gotten over her morning sickness, but I think the real reason was she was ashamed now that everybody was talking about her, calling her fast and worse.

We were all alone. Our apartment was an unmoored desert island that was floating farther out to sea each day. Nobody came by to get their hair pressed and curled anymore. Even if Mama had felt like doing her kitchen beautician work, she couldn't because the smell of fried hair was one of the things that made Chantelle puke. Daddy was still mad at Miss Donna and the other women and wouldn't allow them to set foot in our house. Other than Sister Calley and Norman, nobody came to visit us except for Ol' Bad Richard and he never came inside. We got so used to being alone that we froze when somebody cop-pounded our door late one night. It took Daddy just a couple of long steps to cross the room and snatch open the door.

Juanita stood there in a full-length fur coat, holding a lit cigarette out from her body like an afterthought. "There's some stuff for the girls downstairs in the car," she announced before turning and going back down the stairs.

Daddy shrugged on his coat and went outside. Mama didn't move. Me and Chantelle took our places side by side at our bedroom window. Just below us a man leaned against the hood of the Cadillac Juanita had been driving the night I tried to save Jessie Mae. The man was big and tall. He could have played Santa Claus if he had wanted to, but he was dressed all wrong. His burgundy shoes matched his suit and his gray overcoat matched his hat.

"Big Josh," Chantelle whispered.

Now after everything, he was just Josh to me.

Josh stood up straight when Daddy stepped out of the entry. He stuck out his hand when Daddy got close enough to shake. Daddy looked down at Josh's hand, and then up toward our window. About twelve hours later, he raised his hand and let Josh shake it. Josh said something to Daddy that we couldn't hear, then went to the rear of the car. Daddy didn't move. Josh jerked open the car trunk, throwing his arms in the air as he did like he was a magician saying, "Tra la!"

Daddy was a rock, a chunk of concrete, a piece of wood. He didn't move. Juanita nudged him toward the trunk. Daddy shrugged and let her lead him to where Josh stood looking hopeful. Josh reached into the trunk and pulled out some packages and handed them to Daddy. When he pulled out the bike, something sucked all of the air out of me. I felt like I had been thrust into the Twilight Zone and was falling, tumbling head over heels, crashing through a big hole in space in a twisted ending to a really sad story.

Chantelle bolted to the living room and was waiting for the two daddies and Juanita when they got there. I was having a hard time getting my legs to work.

"Where's Bernie?"

"Here I am, Daddy."

Daddy took a deep breath and said, "Baby girls, I want you to meet . . ."

"Uncle Josh," the man said.

Chantelle momentarily lapsed back into stupid and asked, "On which side?"

Josh winked at her. "Both sides," he said. "I brought y'all a li'l something for the holiday season."

Juanita took the packages from Daddy and handed them to Chantelle. Josh smiled in my direction, and kinda shoved the bike at me. It was pink with handlebar tassels that sparkled in the dim light. A cutesy little wicker basket with ribbon threaded through it hung from the handlebars. I didn't reach for it. It would have fallen if Daddy hadn't grabbed it. I squeezed my eyes shut and fought for my balance.

A classic case of too little too late.

Juanita's words lashed at me, their sharp edges striking at tender places, dicing me into little pieces. The pieces did not hold. My arms got all floppy. My legs stopped working. I slid to the floor. For a moment I thought I had melted. Chantelle's mouth flew open in the shape of a scream, but no sound came out. Mama's mouth was moving. Daddy's mouth was moving. I remember thinking, "How strange, they've suddenly lost their voices."

I lay where they had placed me earlier that night when my legs had stopped working—dead center of my bed with the covers pulled up to my chin and tucked around me as tight as a crimped pie crust.

Helicoptering blades of light slashed across my closed lids, jolting me awake. Sirens wailed in the distance.

Chantelle was up patting the wall, trying to find the light switch.

"Leave the light alone!"

"Mama . . .?"

"Just do what I said. Get back in bed!" Mama's words were quick and sharp.

"But, Mama—"

"Child . . ." Mama warned.

Chantelle made a sniffling sound and returned to her bed. I wanted to go to her and rub her back and tell her not to cry, but Mama had put a spell on me and I couldn't separate myself from the inside of my bed pie.

Someone was beating on our front door, beating so hard I expected to hear the hinges give and wood splinter, any minute. I don't know how and I don't know why, but right away, I knew something had happened to Daddy. "Where's Daddy?" I whispered.

Mama didn't answer. I raised my voice. I was almost shouting.

"Where's my Daddy?"

Mama made a sound like a snake getting ready to strike and called my name. I knew to be quiet. Chantelle was still sniffling. She was confused and scared. So was I. I wanted my Daddy. I wanted him so bad I could taste it. I didn't want him to kill anybody, anymore. I just wanted him to be my daddy.

I'm so sorry, Daddy. Please forgive me.

"Stay in the bed, no matter what. Don't say anything, to anybody, no matter what. Don't say a word."

"Where's Daddy?"

"Bernadine, just do what I say."

Then she left, and I heard her at the front door. "Who is it?"

"Police. Open up."

I heard the front door open, then the movement of heavy footsteps, and short bursts of cackling static.

153

"Any men in this unit, ma'am?" one set of footsteps asked. The other footsteps were everywhere. I could hear them going down the hall and out in the kitchen.

"No suh, um sorry to say there ain't—at least not tonight."

"Does a man live here?"

"No suh—well off and on, but not right now. Ain't nobody here but me and my chil'ren."

"We're going to need to search, ma'am."

"Hep yo'self. I ain't got nothin' to hide."

Our door swung open. A blast of light swept across the room and settled on us.

"Dem's my chil'ren."

"Where's their daddy?"

"Got they behinds in the wind. Welfare lady scared 'em off."

Cop nudged my foot with his stick. "Hey gal, where's your pappy hiding?"

Mama said, "She not right in the head. She don't talk. The one by the window—she sick."

The other set of footsteps stopped outside the bedroom door. "Nothing back there," he said to his partner.

"Better check under their beds."

I heard weight shifting and leather creaking and then, "Nothing there."

"Ma'am, do you own a car?"

"Yes, suh, I surely do. A '53 Plymouth. Bought from the lady I work for."

Something about the way Mama was talking made me feel dirty, cheap.

"Is the license plate number 7L1456?"

"That sounds 'bout right."

"Ma'am, where is your car?"

154

"It's parked right out there under the window."

"Would you point it out to me?"

"Wait a minute . . . did them kids take it again? Them joyriders—that why ya'll here?"

"Show us your car."

Mama squeezed past our beds and went to the window. She stood there looking out on the street a long time before turning back to the room. "Um gonna skin those li'l heathens!"

"Who did you let have your car tonight?"

"Nobody. Them kids must'a took it."

"What kids?"

"Joyriders, like I told you. This ain't the first time."

"I find out different, I'm coming back. You understand?"

"Yes, suh."

"If I come back your black ass is going to jail. You understand?'

"Yes, suh, ah unnerstan'."

Mama locked the door behind the police and came back to our room. She stood to the side of the window, so she could look out into the street without being seen.

"Where's Daddy?"

Mama sighed. "Something's happened—"

The thought of something happening to Daddy propelled me up out of my bed.

"Your Daddy's okay, right now. But something happened further down in West Oakland"

"What was Daddy doing there?" Chantelle, still without a clue, wanted to know.

"He and Norman were out on a fool's errand."

"Doing what, Mama?"

"Ask your sister."

I could feel Chantelle turn toward me in the dark.

"Looking for the Sheik?" I asked.

"Yes, Bernadine," Mama said, "looking for the Sheik."

Chantelle wailed softly in her bed.

"I told you, Bernadine, if you kept on acting pitiful you were going to goad your daddy into doing something he would regret."

"But Mama, I wasn't acting."

"Shut up, Bernadine. Just shut up."

"What about Norman, Mama. He okay?" Chantelle asked.

Mama busied herself peeking out the window without responding.

"Is Norman okay?"

Mama sighed. "I don't know," she said.

A soft keening rose from Chantelle's bed. I climbed into her bed and held her in my arms.

I said, "It's alright, Chantelle. Don't cry." But I was crying too.

Mama shushed us and turned back to the window.

CHAPTER 23

Mama had stretched the phone cord all the way into our room. She stood hunched over, whispering into the receiver, as she peeked out the window. She hung up. Then she turned to us, lying stiff and scared in our beds, and whispered rapid-fire instructions.

"I want you both to get up—I don't want any lip. Don't make any noise. Leave the lights off. Put on your shoes—forget the socks—and throw your coats on over your nightclothes. Get a move on!"

Choking back a thousand questions about Daddy, about Norman, about where we were going in the middle of the night and why, we got up and did what Mama told us. I was worried that my legs still weren't working, but the floor felt firm when my feet touched it, and when I stood up my legs held me alright. Chantelle was moving slow and stiff like a zombie. I fished her shoes from under the bed and slipped her feet into them.

Although I had been lying wide awake, too scared to close my eyes since the police left, this still felt like a dream. I bit the inside of my lip, and though it hurt, I knew that didn't mean anything. Dreams can be tricky. They have a habit of cheating on tests. And just like that, from out of nowhere, the thought hit me again: Daddy really is dead. We're going to view his body. That's why Mama's acting all spooky. Daddy is dead, and it's all my fault. I moaned. The floor skittered out from under me, and I fell across the bed. Mama grabbed a fist full of my gown and snatched me up. I was about an inch from her face.

"I'm not going to have any of that out of you, Bernadine," she said through gritted teeth. "Not now. You hear me? Your daddy wants to see you before he leaves. I'm telling you now, I will break your neck if you act a fool and get him caught."

"Daddy's not dead?" I whispered.

"No, your daddy's not dead, but he's likely to be if the police get their hands on him. Now, get your ass up."

I struggled into my coat and helped Chantelle with hers. We went single file with Mama in front, Chantelle in the middle, and me on the end, through the living room and into the kitchen. Mama paused before opening the back door.

"Listen," she said, "there's a police car parked out front. We have to make it down to Donna's without them knowing."

Chantelle squeezed past Mama to the door. "Let me open it, she said. "I know how to do it so it won't squeak." Mama stood back. Chantelle grabbed the doorknob with both hands and lifted the door as she turned the knob. The door opened silently. Mama couldn't resist a soft, knowing "Um huh" as we stepped out into the dark. The cold bit at our bare legs. The garbage stank. Broken glass crunched under our feet.

We made it down the stairs without clanging on the metal steps and huddled in the shadows, peering out at the buildings grouped around the courtyard. The entrances to the buildings were black holes—not one was lit. There should have been a naked bulb swinging from the ceiling of every landing in each entrance but not tonight. Either every bulb had died at precisely the same moment or somebody had taken a stick and systematically smashed each and every one them. Nobody was about, not somebody's daddy coming home from the late shift, not bad kids playing Hide and Go Get It, not the doo-woppers, not the Grove Street College Boys. Nobody. It was so quiet I could hear trucks rumbling down Highway 80 blocks away. Chestnut Court had never been that quiet.

Mama took a deep breath and held it for a while. She let it out slowly, and then slipped out of the entrance. Flattening her back against the outside wall of our building, she inched along, feeling her way with the palms of her hands. We followed, doing the same. Funny smelling, prickly bushes with little purple berries grew along the walls. We squeezed in between them and the wall. Sticking and stinging any part of our bodies that weren't covered, the bushes tore us up but they were the only place we had to hide. We had made it half way to the next entrance when we heard the car. It could have been down the street or a block away—we couldn't tell. My racing heart told me it was only inches away. We froze and tried to flatten ourselves against the building even more. Chantelle was trembling. I grabbed her hand and squeezed it hard. She squeezed back and her trembling stopped.

"Get down!" Mama hissed. We dropped to our knees, hunching down with our hands locked over our heads, the way they taught us to do in school in case the Russians dropped an atom bomb on us. We stayed like that, trying real hard to look like a cluster of stinky bushes and straining to hear where the car was. All we could tell was that it was close. Then it was very close. We could hear the slow rolling tires crunching dried leaves and old bottle caps and the engine making a sound between a whine and a growl.

Here come the paddyrollers.

I searched myself, did a kind of inventory, trying to figure out what I had left to fight with. I didn't have Artie's chain to swing. I thought wistfully of what I could do with a stick of dynamite or one of Audie Murphy's hand grenades. I never thought about running. I was too tired to run. Besides, I couldn't leave my mama and my sister to fend for themselves.

The engine's whine changed, and I realized the car had stopped. All I could think about was how I was going to protect my mama and my sister. Out the corner of my eye, I could see a police car stopped at our entrance—the one we had just left. One minute the entrance was dark, and the next it blazed like a supernova, as the police blasted it

159

with the searchlight mounted to the top of the patrol car.

They saw us! They saw us! How could they not see us?

I think Chantelle would have bolted if Mama hadn't whispered her name. The light went off just as suddenly as it had come on, and the patrol car started moving again. It slowed down again when it was almost opposite us. We stayed where we were, willing ourselves to be unseen. Finally the car rolled past us to the next entrance where it stopped and blasted it with light. We allowed ourselves to breathe again, but we didn't move.

The police car rolled to the next entrance, Miss Donna's entrance, and I sensed mama tense up. The searchlight revealed nothing of interest there and the car rolled on, stopping and repeating its ritual at the next two entrances before turning out of the courtyard onto Chestnut Street.

We climbed out of the bushes and walked/ran to Miss Donna's. She opened the door before we could knock.

Mama pushed past Miss Donna's and went straight through the kitchen to the living room. Artie was there and so was his mother, Miss Bea. But Mama paid as much attention to them as she did to the furniture. Mama scanned the room looking for Daddy. I did too. I tried to keep my face blank. I didn't want anybody to know how scared I was that I might never see him again. When Mama didn't find Daddy, she whirled around to Miss Donna who stood quietly behind her. Before Mama could say anything, Miss Donna grabbed her in a bear hug and held her tight. Mama struggled for a moment, and then collapsed into Miss Donna's arms. Miss Donna held Mama until it was okay to let her go.

"My husband . . ." Mama whispered,

"He's alright for now. I'll go get him as soon as it's safe."

A faint "whoop whoop" floated in from somewhere outside.

"The coast is clear," Artie announced. Miss Donna disappeared out the back door.

Daddy smelled like smoke and garbage when he stole in through the back door, followed by Miss Donna. Mama grabbed him and hugged him like she was never going to let go. Me and Chantelle grabbed what we could—a piece of arm, a shoulder, a hand—and hung on with absolutely no intention of ever letting go.

Mama said, "Alex, I've loved you since the day I met you . . ."

"I know, baby, I know. Take care of my girls, okay."

"Alex . . ."

I could feel Mama struggling with herself, fighting against the urge to beg Daddy not to go. Daddy could feel it too.

"I won't be gone long, baby. Promise. Just got to let this mess die down some."

Daddy adjusted his arms so me and Chantelle could squeeze into his hug. He looked at Chantelle and then at me and sighed. He opened his mouth to speak, then closed it again. It seemed like he was trying to find just the right thing to say, a thirty-second version of everything we would ever need to know that could only be told to us by a daddy. Finally, he said to Chantelle, "No matter what, you finish your education. Hear me?" Chantelle nodded. "Take care of my grand-baby." She nodded again. Daddy kissed her on the forehead. Turning to me he said, "Don't forget to take those books back to the library before . . ." He couldn't finish because by then he was crying. "Before . . ." He gave up and kissed my forehead. As he did, he whispered, "You have everything you will ever need." I choked back a sob. It felt like my chest was going to explode. Soon I wouldn't have Daddy. How could that be everything? But I nodded and said, "Okay, Daddy."

"You girls are my heart. You are just as good as anybody else. You hear me? Don't let anybody tell you different. You deserve good things in your lives."

Miss Donna touched Daddy's shoulder. "Better get going now."

Daddy had to let us go.

Miss Bea pulled a baby sock out of her bosom. It was a pink, stretchy kind—a money sock with the top tied in a knot.

"Forty-nine dollars and forty-nine cents—seven times seven," she said, "for luck, and a piece of High John the Conqueror root for everything else."

Although Daddy didn't believe in all of that hoodoo stuff, he took the sock and thanked Miss Bea.

Mama reached in her coat pocket and took out something heavy wrapped in a diaper. It was the gun. Daddy took it from Mama and shoved it into his jacket pocket. "Donna, will you help Vonda pick up something? I don't want my girls to be left without protection."

Miss Donna nodded.

Artie had been standing with his head cocked to one side. He blinked his eyes like he was doing a math problem in his head. He took an old man's watch on a chain out of his pocket and stared down at it. He dropped his hand and said, "Now! You got two minutes. The bike's under the stairs."

Daddy headed for the front door.

"Where y'all going?" Miss Donna demanded when Mama, and me and Chantelle, lined up at the door behind him.

Nobody answered.

"Y'all gone get the man shot!"

Daddy turned around and mouthed a silent plea to us. Mama nodded and stepped back. Daddy opened the door a little and slipped out. We went to the window and peered through Miss Donna's blinds without touching them so there would be no movement to attract attention.

I heard a couple of soft "whoops" and then Artie exclaim, "What?" like he was having a conversation with somebody who had just told him something astonishing. "Cops coming," he said.

We swung around from the window to stare at Artie like he could control what was happening if he tried hard enough.

A dog barked, and then there were the "whoops" again.

"They coming this way from Twenty-Fourth Street."

I was scared for Daddy, and I was sad for myself. Then I was sad for Daddy. Then I was sad for Chantelle and for Mama. I was sad for Chantelle's baby and for Sister Calley. Then, after a while, I wasn't sad or scared. I was calm. I had to save my daddy.

I unbuttoned my coat and let it slip to the floor without anybody in the darkened room noticing. Taking great care to remain unnoticed, I scrubbed off my right shoe using my left foot and then scrubbed off the other shoe the same way. I stood barefoot and liberated in nothing but my nightgown. I drew in a deep breath slowly and held it. I let it out slowly. Then I bolted for the door.

The cold night air slammed into me just as shock exploded in the room behind me. There was a collective sharp intake of breath and then frantic scrambling. I heard Mama call my name but I didn't stop. I propelled myself down the stairs so quickly I felt I was flying.

Daddy stood toward the back of the entrance in the darkness that the streetlight couldn't reach, his hand jammed in the pocket where he had stuffed the gun. I heard Mama call my name again as I leaped over the last two steps and bolted into the night.

Don't follow me, Daddy. Please don't follow me.

Driving slowly on the wrong side of the street, the police were back to checking entrances. I ran directly at them, screaming at the top of my lungs, "I didn't steal yo money! Why you always blaming me?"

I could hear Mama behind me, "Bring your ass back here!"

I ran straight for the police car, straight into the beam of its headlights, straight toward the driver like he had some kind of fishing line and was reeling me in. The police car lurched to a stop just as I slammed into the front bumper and hit the ground. I scrambled to my feet and ran around to the driver's side and scratched at his door, trying to open it. "Let me in," I pleaded. She gon' whup me!"

Before the police could move, Mama cut through their light.

"Bring you ass back here," she screamed.

"I didn't do it!"

The light from the police car found us. *Good. They're turning to follow us.* I was almost at the corner before I couldn't run anymore, and Mama caught up with me. She grabbed me by my wrist, took off one shoe, held it by the heel, and beat the mess out of me with it, as I screamed for the police.

"Alright, alright, what's going on here?"

"This—child—has—a—bad—habit of stealing from my purse." Mama said through gritted teeth, accenting every other word with a vicious whack from the shoe.

I responded with another, "I didn't do it."

The police chuckled. "You better take that on inside."

Mama whacked me a couple more times before dragging me toward the entrance farthest from Miss Donna's. The police followed us until we cut back into Chestnut Court. Then they sped up and continued about their business.

Mama didn't let up with the swats. "Don't you ever do anything like that again, you fool-assed girl," she repeated every few feet as she dragged me back to Miss Donna's.

"We had to wrestle him down to keep him from going out there after his li'l girl with that gun in his pocket. Took all three of us to hold him back."

"Did he get away okay?"

"Finally. Even after he figured out that you all were trying to distract the police, he still didn't want to go. We did all we could to convince him"

Back in my coat and shoes with one of Miss Donna's blankets wrapped around me, I sat at the kitchen table hunched over a cup of warm milk. I don't like warmed milk, but milk was a whole lot better than Mama's tea. And Miss Donna was being so kind, so I took a small sip.

Mama stood towering over me. She was in her position of command—hands on hips, elbows out, shoulders bunched. "Have you lost your mind?"

I considered her question. I had nothing else to lose. Nothing to gain, for that matter, except for my daddy's safety. I couldn't help Jessie Mae escape, but I had succeeded with my daddy. The one person I needed in my life more than anyone else was gone.

Mama stared down at me for a long time. She cocked her head to the side and studied me, evaluated me. She breathed in deeply, almost like she was trying to get a taste of me. Then she turned away, but not quick enough. Not before I saw the corners of her mouth twitch into the teeniest smile.

CHAPTER 24

Miss Bea anointed Chantelle's forehead and the tender parts of her wrists with some holy oil that was supposed to protect Chantelle and keep her and the baby safe. Placing both hands on Chantelle's shoulders, Miss Bea held her at arm's length and studied her. "It's going to be a boy," she announced, and Chantelle smiled for the first time in a long time. "It is foretold that he will do great things. For it is He who will rise up and lead our people to their true freedom."

Sensing that Miss Bea was on the verge of launching into one of her sermons that she was so famous for in Chestnut Court, Artie whispered, "Ma'dear, we gotta go now."

Miss Bea bit her lower lip and nodded. She kissed Chantelle on both cheeks, held her by her shoulders again, and sought out Chantelle's eyes.

"Remember, baby, the Lord never gives us more than we can bear."

Chantelle looked confused, but she held Miss Bea's gaze and nodded. Miss Donna hustled Miss Bea and Artie out the back door. Chantelle turned to Mama with a questioning look. Mama sucked in her bottom lip and bit down on it the way you do when you're trying to keep from screaming.

Miss Donna crossed her arms over her chest. "Ain't no way I'm going to let you all go back to your place, not after everything."

Mama didn't argue. None of us wanted to go back to the apartment and be reminded that Daddy wasn't there, and that we didn't know when or even if he would ever come back. There was a lot of scrambling about getting blankets and pillows, and deciding who would sleep where.

"Vonnie, you and Chantelle can sleep in my bed. Bernie, I'll make up a nice comfy spot on the couch for you, and I—she shuddered because one or both (it was hard to tell which since they slept together) peed the bed—will sleep with Max and Sherry."

"Why Chantelle gets to sleep with Mama?" I wanted to strangle myself the minute that question escaped my mouth. I sounded like such a baby. But Daddy was gone, and all I had left was Mama. I didn't need Chantelle hogging her.

I expected something tart from Mama's mouth, but all she said was, "Can we make a pallet for her in the room with us?"

"Sure," Miss Donna said with a strange sort of forced cheerfulness. That's cool. Now I get the couch."

Whenever Swan's Discount Department Store had a sale, Miss Donna stocked up on whatever was offered, buying boxes and sometimes crates of stuff to use herself but mostly to sell to neighbors. Run out of baking powder and the corner store is closed? Send a kid to Miss Donna's to buy some from her. Run out of tissue paper in the middle of the night? Miss Donna has some in stock. Miss Donna's four-poster bed sat amid a sea of cellophane bags of toilet tissue, five-pound cans of coffee stacked four high, a hundred pound bag of pinto beans, a push lawn mower, and numerous unmarked bags and cardboard boxes. We crammed my pallet in a landlocked space between the window and the bed. If I needed to go to the bathroom, I would have to crawl across the foot of the bed to get to the door.

Mama and Chantelle sat with their backs against the headboard. My throat tightened when Mama put her arm around Chantelle and drew her in close. "Chantelle, she said, "I'm going to tell you something, something very important, and I want you to listen carefully. Okay?"

Chantelle looked up at Mama and nodded.

Mama continued. "When you're carrying a baby, some people think you get weak, that you suddenly become delicate and frail. But that's not true, not true at all. You grow stronger. Your back gets stronger. Your hands get stronger. Your bones become like steel. If they cooked you and tried to eat you, your flesh would be too tough to chew. You grow stronger because that is what is needed. If you needed to fly you would grow wings."

Mama looked down at Chantelle. "You understand me, Chantelle?"

After a few seconds, Chantelle nodded.

"You know what else happens? Your mind gets sharper. You develop the ability to think through, under, and around obstacles. You think minutes ahead, hours ahead, even years ahead. You outthink the devil and all of his imps. You understand me?"

Chantelle didn't answer. It seemed like she was holding her breath, waiting for the rest of what Mama was building up to.

Mama's voice softened. "Your heart grows stronger. It beats hard and strong because you insist on it. You insist that your heart doesn't let up on its job, that it keeps pumping life blood to you and your baby."

"Mama . . .?"

Rushing to finish before she lost the will, Mama continued: "You are a woman now. And sometimes women must face tough things. I want you to remember that no matter how tough things get I will always be your mama. You always have me to lean on. And there's nothing so tough that we can't face it together."

There was tenderness in Mama's voice, but an insistence too, a barely discernable demand that Chantelle let go of whatever bound her to childhood, that she cross the divide from childish expectations of joy over to the ranks of strong women who bore woe willfully.

The streetlight caught Mama's face, and I could see that it was slick with silent tears. I don't know if I was crying too, but my throat was raw, and it felt like it was closing up on me.

"Mama . . ."

"Yes, Chantelle."

"It's about Norman?"

Mama nodded. "Baby, Norman is dead. The police killed him."

I expected Chantelle to scream or something. It just wasn't her to suffer quietly. But she sat still as a rock. Someone in the room was crying, making such a pitiful snot-choking sound. It was some time before I realized that someone was me. Mama reached down and dragged me up onto the foot of the bed. I hugged the lump her knees made under the covers, buried my face in it, and cried like a baby. People are always talking about "broken heart" this and "broken heart" that, but let me tell you, it's not just the heart that breaks. Your eyes scale over, stop working, and you go blind; your lungs seize up, stealing your breath away; your stomach somehow finds glass to grind; your skull cracks open, letting flies get at your brain; and for one tiny second, you wish you were dead too.

"Breathe, Chantelle! Breathe!" Mama sounded frantic.

Chantelle's head flopped about as Mama shook her. Mama shouted for Miss Donna. She rushed in, carrying an ammonia-soaked rag. Mama grabbed it and jammed it under Chantelle's nose. Swinging her arms wildly and jerking her head from side to side, Chantelle tried to fight off breathing, but the ammonia did its job.

"That's all I know, baby. They were driving around down by our old house, and the police stopped them for something—I don't know what—maybe nothing. They put your daddy in the back of one of their cars, and tried to put Norman in another, but he refused, demanding to know what they were charging them with. Things got ugly. The police started beating on him."

Chantelle sucked in a gulp of air and made a sound like she was going to start crying. But she didn't, instead she hummed something tuneless.

Mama whispered, "It's alright to cry, baby."

Arms wrapped across her chest as though in a straightjacket, Chantelle nodded but continued to hum softly, rocking like she was trying to put herself to sleep.

"Folks came pouring out of those old, supposedly abandoned houses to take the 'brothers' back, to so-call 'liberate' them. They got to fighting the police. They say the police set fire to one of the houses, and just about all of them went up in flames."

"Ours too?"

"I don't know. But a lot of them burned down. They got your daddy out of the back seat of that police car, and a few of them turned it over and set it on fire. The police started shooting. Your daddy managed to get away."

"He left Norman?"

"No, baby, some of Norman's friends took him away. Alex knew Norman had been shot but he didn't know how bad it was. He didn't know Norman would bleed to death before they could get him to Highland. Your daddy had to leave the car. That's why the police came to our house looking for him."

"What are we going to do now, Mama?"

"We're going to do what we're supposed to do, Bernadine. You and Chantelle are going back to school, and I'm going back to work. I do my job, and you two do yours. We'll be alright."

"It won't be alright! We need Daddy."

"Well, we don't have him. We'll have to make do. And Bernie, hang on to your childhood as long as you can, as long as we can afford for you to. Stop trying to be so womanish. Being grown isn't that easy."

"You think being a kid is?"

At times my chest would hurt. It got tender in spots. Chantelle said they were on their way—my titties. But, by then, titties were the last thing on my mind. I spent most of my time thinking about Daddy. At night, when I was getting ready for bed, I'd wonder if he was getting ready for bed, too. In the morning, when I was getting ready for school, I'd wonder if Daddy was already up, if he'd had his coffee the way he likes it with two teaspoons of sugar and a little PET Milk. I wondered if he was thinking about me, if he missed me. I wondered how long it would be before he could come home. Sometimes I thought about Jessie Mae, but not as much as I used to. I wondered what life would have been like if I had saved her, helped her get away down South to her grandmother. Would Norman still be alive? Would Daddy have had to leave?

But, I stopped dreaming about Jessie Mae.

Even though Daddy was gone, Mama stopped whuppin me.

And, I was never afraid of movie monsters again.

Made in the USA
Lexington, KY
17 December 2013